PIGALLE PALACE

Dear Reader:

What is a Strebor Quickiez? Years ago, I decided that I wanted to create a series of short, erotic books that would be designed to be read in the span of one day. Thus, the Strebor Quickiez collection was born. Whether a reader takes in the excitement on the way to and from work on public transportation, or during their lunch break and before bedtime, they can get a "quick fix" in the form of a stimulating read.

Strebor Quickiez will be enticing to those who steer away from larger novels and those who do not have the time to commit to spend a longer while taking in a good read.

It is my hope and desire that booksellers embrace Strebor Quickiez and promote them to their consumer base. I am convinced that these books can do a heavy volume in sales and, as always, I appreciate the support shown to all of my efforts throughout the years.

Blessings,

Zane

Publisher
Strebor Books
www.simonandschuster.com

PIGALLE PALACE

A NOVEL

NIYAH MOORE

STREBOR BOOKS

NEW YORK LONDON TORONTO SYDNEY

Strebor Books
P.O. Box 6505
Largo, MD 20792
http://www.streborbooks.com

This book is a work of fiction. Names, characters, places and incidents are products of the author's imagination or are used fictitiously. Any resemblance to actual events or locales or persons, living or dead, is entirely coincidental.

ISBN 978-1-59309-632-8
ISBN 978-1-4767-8332-1 (ebook)
LCCN 2014942329

First Strebor Books trade paperback edition March 2015

Cover design: www.mariondesigns.com
Cover photograph: © Keith Saunders/Keith Saunders Photos

10 9 8 7 6 5 4 3 2 1

Manufactured in the United States of America

For information regarding special discounts for bulk purchases, please contact Simon & Schuster Special Sales at 1-866-506-1949 or business@simonandschuster.com

The Simon & Schuster Speakers Bureau can bring authors to your live event. For more information or to book an event, contact the Simon & Schuster Speakers Bureau at 1-866-248-3049 or visit our website at www.simonspeakers.com.

Dedicated to Londyn Lashaye Bosley

ACKNOWLEDGMENTS

First and foremost, I want to thank God because without him, I wouldn't be blessed with the talents that he has given me. I know that within an instant, it can be taken away. His love for me goes beyond any measure. To my future husband, Malcolm, thank you for loving me. You are an amazing man and don't you forget that. To my kids, Ciera, Cameron, and my angel in heaven, Londyn, I love you guys. My parents, sisters, and brother—I love you guys. To my enormous family of aunts, uncles, and cousins—I love you guys, too. To all my friends, thank you for being there when I needed you.

I want to send a special shout-out to my literary family: Zane, N'Tyse, Karen E. Quinones Miller, Shakir Rashaan, David Weaver, Carla Pennington, Porscha Sterling, Royalty Publishing House as a whole, and SBR Publications. I'm so glad that I have connected with you all. I love everyone that crosses my path, but you all have a special place in my heart.

I want to thank all the reviewers and all of the readers that have taken the time to let me know that you are out there reading my work. Without your feedback, I wouldn't be able to grow as an artist. I'm very passionate about my writing and I'm glad that you enjoy it.

Thank you ALL from the bottom of my heart.

CHAPTER 1

LEGEND

She clutched my back, digging her nails into me every time I thrust into her. I loved giving every woman I chose the ultimate pleasure and I couldn't stop from thinking about how good she felt as her sticky walls hugged me. Sinking my teeth into her skin was the other thing that came to my mind, but I didn't want to suck her blood…not yet anyway. I actually hadn't made up my mind if I wanted to feed off her. Her sex seemed satisfying enough not to, and my vampire instincts weren't pulling me in that direction.

After a few more deep long pumps from me, she drew in deep shallow breaths, let go of the death grip she had on my back, and thanked God aloud for one hell of an orgasm.

"Are you okay?" I asked her after I watched her mild trembles subside.

"I'm fine," she exasperated with her eyes wide in amazement.

"Would you like anything else tonight?"

She played in my dreads as she admired my body with her free hand. "Can you make me another Lemon Drop?"

At the bar, earlier that evening, she and her best friend had indulged in the drinks I served them. As a bartender, I met beautiful women by the dozens every night. Most of the faces were familiar, and on occasion, tourists showed up.

"Your Lemon Drop is coming right up." I eased off her.

When she smiled at me, I thought she was stunning, too cute for words. I thought that about her all night long. Before I brought her home from Club Vaisseau, I admired her honey-colored skin, medium-brown, doe-like eyes, and long dark hair from the other side of the bar.

I recognized any type of freak, regardless of what type of clothing she wore. This one was so freaky that she allowed me to sex her before even knowing her name. Typical for me, though. One-night stands weren't a rare event on my calendar. I needed many women to quench my desire for sex the way quarts of blood satisfied my hunger.

I draped my bare body in a bathrobe. "Mademoiselle, pardon me, but what's your name?"

She giggled sexily, yet I could tell that she, too, felt embarrassed about not exchanging that information earlier. "Chantal."

"You're really beautiful, Chantal. It's been a pleasure having your company tonight."

She blushed and stammered, "T-t-t-hanks."

"Don't move, and um, keep those clothes off." Holding up my index finger, I signaled for her to wait while I went downstairs to make her another Lemon Drop.

Chantal giggled again, the way a schoolchild did when told a dirty joke. She didn't have to play the shy role anymore. I had already gotten what I needed from her, but my mere presence had her still feeling shy. Hell, it made all women act that way whenever they were around me. That was my gift and my curse—to capture a woman effortlessly.

I swiftly made her sweet lemon concoction, and was back upstairs in a flash.

"You move fast," she said with a bright smile.

All vampires moved fast. However, she hadn't noticed my fangs because I hid them well around humans. I only revealed them when I was ready to drink. By then, the hypnotic state masked my intentions.

I handed her the Lemon Drop while my eyes peered down at her curvy body.

"Thank you, Mr. ...?"

I hadn't told her my name, either.

"Please, call me Legend."

"Legend? Is that your real name?"

"It's the only name I know."

She stared at me oddly, as she took a few sips from the glass. "I have to pee." As she got up from the bed, her thick hips grazed against me.

I grunted lowly, while falling back on the bed, feeling happy with having her over for the night.

When she finished relieving her bladder, she asked, "Legend?"

"What's up, Chantal?"

"How come your skin is so cold?" She stood in front of the bed with a look of bewilderment.

"My skin is cold?" I repeated as if I didn't know that I wasn't warm-blooded.

Warm blood hadn't run through me for over a century.

She hesitated as her eyes glanced over me nervously. I could tell her mind was trying to put the pieces together and recollect if she'd noticed any other strange things throughout the evening.

Chantal had come to the bar with her friend, and whether or not they were aware, it was no accident how they'd ended up in Pigalle Palace or even in the Red Light District, for that matter. The Red Light District was devoted to prostitution and other illegal, immoral behavior. The Red Light District was heavy in sexual acts.

Therefore, our meeting was no accident.

Whether pussy was bought, sold, or given freely, it was our haven nonetheless.

Our popular thriving nightclub, Vaisseau, was one of the many notorious hotspots. Pigalle Palace was an epicenter of sizzling sex shops, erotic peep shows, and dazzling strip clubs. It was an adults-only, X-rated pleasurable adventure for the more risqué crowd and home to one of Paris' most famous cabarets, Moulin Rouge.

This was our playground and Chantal was having a ball. In the back of her mind, she had already known what I was and that excited her.

Speechless for a second, she finally replied, "Now that I'm thinking about it, from the moment your lips touched mine at the club, I noticed. I noticed something different about you all night. I've heard many things about Pigalle Palace. Let me say that you were the one that catapulted my curiosity further. I finally got to touch *one* up close and very personal."

"*One of what?*"

A quick frown appeared on her face, yet she continued, "Are you going to bite me now?"

What had me confused was that she looked as if she were disappointed that I hadn't taken a bite out of her yet. "You want me to bite you?"

Chantal straddled me and ran her feather-feeling hands across my chest. "Am I not worthy enough?"

"Are you not worthy enough to be killed?"

Her eyes widened with fear. "Oh no, no, no. I don't want you to kill me. Are you going to kill me? I hope you don't kill me…"

"What do you want from me, Chantal?"

"I want you to turn me into what it is that you are."

The way her eyes sparkled when she suggested such a ridiculous thing made me stare deeply into her eyes. I wasn't going to hypnotize or compel her. I simply didn't know many humans that wanted to become what we were. Hell, we didn't want to either, but we had no other choice.

"I'm very careful and *we* don't change anyone unless it's discussed amongst the family first."

"Have you ever changed anyone behind their backs?"

I got very serious on her. "Legend follows all rules."

"Is that the only reason why you haven't taken my blood, Legend?"

Instantly, I wanted to kill her. When she mentioned blood, it triggered my hunter instincts, and I wanted to suck her until she became lifeless.

I dismissed the urge. "You don't want me to answer that."

She gasped with fascination. "Can I see your fangs?"

I tilted my head back a bit so she could see what she was begging for.

"Wow. Legend, you are truly a vampire. My assumption was correct all along."

"And now that you've proven your theory to be correct, what do you want to do?"

I could feel the heat pulsating from her moist center that greeted me so pleasantly. She was excited by her discovery and was ready to open up her body for me again. To be honest, I was turned on as well, but I had to see where she wanted to go with this.

"I want you to have me."

"I've already had you, Chantal."

"Drink from me." She put her wrist up to my nose.

Though she smelled so delicious, I gently lowered her arm and explained, "I've been a vampire for a very long time. This is my destiny, not yours. You should enjoy the fact that you're still alive."

She swallowed hard and thought about that for a moment, but then she was right back to trying to pressure me. "You sure you don't want to bite me?" She tossed her hair over her shoulder to reveal her neck. I spotted a luscious thick vein that I could have devoured if I'd truly wanted to.

"I'm sure."

The urge to bite her surged through me the same way my adrenaline had my blood rushing, but I had self-control.

"Why not?" She began plastering kisses on the side of my face.

"Stop it," I said in a demanding tone.

She backed away with a look of confusion, pushing her hair out of her face with one hand.

My family didn't have a choice. We were born with this curse.

My right eye pulsated as it fluttered. A painful migraine formed. Out of the corner of my eye, I could see Chantal staring at me before sauntering over to the window to look down at the city of Montmartre.

"Oh my... This is a sight to see. I've never seen this side of Paris before..."

I had an excellent panoramic view of the city and it was breathtaking.

"We're on a hill, north of Paris, one hundred thirty metres high."

"The city is so beautiful, Legend."

I got up from the bed and wrapped my arms around her waist. The thought of slipping back inside of her came to mind. Without any distractions, I would be able to enjoy her for a little while longer before the sun would come up. She would then go on her merry little way and her fantasy of spending a complete night with a vampire would be fulfilled.

She twirled around to face me. Her eyes shifted down while sadness seemed to consume her. She was curious about becoming something she didn't understand. Our world was dark and confusing to most, yet she was so ready.

"I've read plenty of vampires' tales and stories."

"That's fiction. I'm real and trust me when I say that you're better off."

"Maybe I should leave."

I stopped her with my voice—smooth, gentle, and reassuring. "Chantal, I'm not done with you, yet. Unless, you're afraid of me now."

"I'm not afraid… Do you always have your way?"

"Always," I stated into the thickened air.

"You sure you don't want to sink your teeth into me? I think I might taste very good."

Her hands moved over my muscles as if she were trying to memorize everything about me.

My hands then moved to her lower back. She closed her eyes as her breathing became heavier. I listened intently, pulling her back to rest up against me while my hands felt around her firm ass. Her breathing grew even heavier with a hint of arousal as my fingertips traveled between her legs to rub her clit. I turned her around, face to face, to inhale her sweet-smelling breath as I inched toward her. I grabbed her firmly, pulled her up against me, and kissed her.

I sucked her neck and then her collarbone, making a suction trail as I led her back to the bed. I pushed her onto her back. She didn't object as I went down to please her. My lips met her warm wetness. She moaned as I sucked her hungrily.

Her low moan began to rise each time I licked her juicy clit. I picked up my slow pace to a moderate rate, feeling her juices squirt and then ooze down between her thighs. I lapped every drop because she tasted that good. By then, she had both fists full of my dreads.

I palmed her ass and squeezed her while her eyes closed tightly. Suddenly her moans stopped and she said, "Ahhhh… Ouch."

As I tasted her blood, I realized I had pierced her inner lips.

"Shit." I tried to get up, but she palmed the back of my head with both of her hands.

"Don't stop… Keep going… Do it."

Without thinking about anything else, I returned my face between her thighs and sucked her blood. Biting her wasn't my intention, but she had aroused me in a way that had me feeling as if I had no control over myself.

Transforming her was something she wanted anyway, so I released my venom and wiped my bloody mouth.

As she had another orgasm, the transformation began. Once her body was done with twisting and writhing in a frantic manner, her sweaty body slid away from me. She didn't cuddle next to me or whisper sweet things as if she loved me for what she'd asked of me all along. Instead, she turned away from me.

I watched her back rise and fall gently as she breathed acutely. I ran my fingers over my dreads as regret washed over me. *What had I done?*

Chantal asked, "How come you couldn't just bite my neck the way I've seen in movies?"

"I wasn't trying to bite you."

"What happens now?"

"The sun will rise. If you decide to walk outside, the sun will touch your skin and you will burn."

She glimpsed over at the window and panicked. "Are you going to close the curtains? I don't want to burn."

"My windows are actually UV protected. You are safe in my home."

A series of electrifying chills shot straight up my spine, creating goose bumps all over my body. I shook the snake-like feeling, heaved a heavy sigh, and closed myself in the bathroom.

My family didn't care about how many women I let into my bed, but the rules were made out to be simple: one was that I could only change one and one only. That one would be my wife for eternity. Those were actually the rules of the covenant. My parents didn't make up those rules. The covenant was made up of laws set by the Préfet—the vampire government of Pigalle Palace.

Before I could gather my thoughts, my phone rang from the countertop of the bathroom. I forgot that I had left it there when I showered. It was my sister, Azura, calling.

My whole family had the gift of premonition. Azura's was the strongest. I knew why she was calling.

"Hello," I answered.

"What are you up to?" Azura asked.

"Nothing much," I tried to elude her.

"Are you planning on leaving home anytime soon?"

"No. The sun will be coming up in a few hours, so I'm in for the night."

"Mother and Father want to see you."

I closed my eyes as I knew exactly why they wanted to see me. "When?"

"Right now."

"Right now?"

"Yes, Legend, right now! Onyx and Rain are already here."

My brothers were already there, so they were aware of what I had done. I was going to have to face them, but I didn't think it would be this soon.

"I'll be there in a moment."

"Hurry," she answered quickly. "Oh, and bring *her* with you."

CHAPTER 2

LEGEND

Our father studied me for a moment as if he couldn't think of anything to say once we arrived at my parents' home. He shifted slightly in the chair in front of the fireplace. I was nervous about what he was going to say. The last thing I wanted to hear was that I was going to have to kill Chantal because I'd broken a rule. Nevertheless, I stood there calmly while Chantal was sprawled out on the couch, completely incoherent to what was going on. The transition of going through the change had that effect.

The whole room was silent. Usually, our father was relaxed and cozy in front of the crackling fire, but his body language as he was sitting up straight, staring me in the eyes without blinking, made me nervous.

That night, the relaxing ability of the open fire wasn't going to soothe the wild beast within him. Since the beginning of our time, we had gathered around the open fire for a sense of safety and deep conversation. We had yet to have one of these meetings as everyone always followed the rules of the covenant.

Father continued to stare through me, rubbing his thick goatee. "You felt the need to do this..."

"I didn't feel the need to do this. It sort of happened."

Regardless of the incident, he was going to pronounce Chantal as my wife, and that was something I really wasn't ready for, but what other choice did I have? I was the idiot who was caught up in the heat of the moment. I was going to have to spend eternity with a woman that I didn't want.

"This *sort of* happened?" Father asked as he observed Chantal.

"Yes."

He cocked his head to the side as if he were trying to figure me out. "You have broken the rules of the covenant and yet, you are so calm about it. You know what this means, don't you?"

"Yes, Father."

"She is now your wife. Is that what you want?"

I was going to have to live with being married to her. Being married now meant that I could never be with another woman again. My days of romping around with plenty of women were over. I was stuck with her. I looked around the room at Azura, Onyx, Rain, and our mother, whom all looked very disappointed in me.

"Yes, Father."

"I should rip her heart out right now."

"No," I replied quickly. "This is my fault, so let me deal with this."

Father leaned his large frame against the living room chair. "Well, I'll tell you what… You take your wife home and make sure she gets the *proper* feeding. We wouldn't want her roaming the district as a newborn. Do I make myself clear?"

"Yes, Father."

He stood up and walked out of the living room.

I sighed under my breath and looked over at Mother.

Mother made a "tsk" sound with her tongue. "*Je pars.*" She said she was leaving in French before following behind him.

Our parents' frustration with me was something I never wanted to cause or see ever again.

"So, are my siblings pissed off with me, too?" I asked them.

Azura stated quickly, "I'm not pissed off; I'm very disappointed. We don't know what kind of wife Chantal will make."

"You mean if she'll become a blood-sucking murderer?"

"Exactly. I guess we'll have to watch and see how she turns out. Let's hope she fights the urges."

Onyx and Rain didn't utter a single word. They didn't have to. I knew my brothers well enough to realize that they had nothing good to say, but their silence left me feeling unsettled. I wanted my siblings to know that everything was going to be fine. Well, that's what I hoped anyway.

I swept up my unconscious bride over my shoulder and left our parents' house without saying anything else to any of them. They would get over it soon, so I decided not to think about it. What was done was done and this mistake would smooth over.

It was about a half an hour too close to the sun rising. I was going to have to hurry home. A few taxis headed my direction. I put my hand out and waved. One taxi finally slowed and pulled up to the curb. I slid Chantal across the new soft leather and a faint smell of strange, unidentifiable funk greeted me. Some cabs carried inimitable odors from either previous riders or the driver. I rolled down the window to get some fresh air to help eliminate some of the stench.

"*Où allez-vous?*" the cab driver asked.

"*Le 18ème arrondissement.*"

He pulled away from the curb smoothly. I lifted my head and stared out of the window as we passed through Montmartre. The sky was still dark, much like the way I was feeling. I had to shake the darkness that was trying to creep over me.

Silently, I sat, but my mind was thinking too loudly. I was such an idiot. My days of conquests were over. Chantal was my wife.

CHAPTER 3

ONYX

The brand-new female bartender we hired was so damned fine that I couldn't stop staring at her. Where had she come from? Azura showed her around our spacious club, spanning more than 45,000 square feet and sprawled across two stories.

Club Vaisseau was ours and it brought a new dimension to the Paris nightlife with its premium location, and breathtaking and lavish décor. It was perfect for a nightlife experience unlike any other and that was the reason why so many flocked our way. We never *ever* hired humans. Living in an all-vampire district, we liked to keep "us" employed. We had plenty of human visitors, but they knew what we were. Those that didn't were usually compelled and lured here by one of us or another vampire.

The new bartender was one of the most beautiful women I had ever seen. I was speechless. We had go-go dancers and peep show girls that worked in our club. I dibbled and dabbled here and there, but there was something different about this one.

Her wild golden hair looked much like a uniformed afro. Her hair brought certain warmth to her cold pale skin, so many would mistake her for a mortal easily. I could tell that when she was human, she had skin the color of toffee. I might've been taking a guess, but I liked to imagine it.

"Who do we have here?" I asked.

"Soleil, this is the middle brother, Onyx. Onyx, this is our brand-new bartender, Soleil," Azura introduced.

"It's a pleasure to meet you, Onyx," Soleil said with a grin.

"Same here," I replied, trying not to smile too hard.

"You're so tall. How tall are you?" she asked, tilting her head back to look into my eyes.

"I'm six-five and you're about five-seven, right?"

"Yeah. You're pretty damned tall. I like your bald head."

I rubbed the top of it with a grin. "Thank you."

"I see why you're the club's door man. Your muscles are pretty... big..."

Azura cleared her throat, catching on to our obvious attraction to one another. "Onyx, Mother needs you to do something for her."

She was trying to interrupt what I was trying to get started, but I went along with it anyway. I smirked. "No problem, sis. I'll head up there now."

While I made my way to the elevator to head to Mother's office, I couldn't shake Soleil's slanted eyes from my mind. I couldn't wait to see how much we had in common.

CHAPTER 4

RAIN

On my way over to Club Vaisseau to work for the night, the raindrops started sprinkling. I was feeling anxious because a good friend of mine, Colette, had told me that she was going to bring a young woman to meet me. See, I had been looking for the perfect woman to spend the rest of my life with and Colette said that she would be.

I stared out of the taxi at all the colorful lights reflecting off the raindrops that remained on the car after the drizzle. In red and blue lights, the signs reading *DVD's*, *Peep Shows*, *Nude*, *New Girls*, and *Sex* surrounded the street. This was home.

Colette called my cell. I picked up. "Hey, Colette."

"Rain. Are you at the club yet?"

"I'm on my way there now."

"Cool. Hey, what you think your parents are going to say when they find out you're pursuing a mortal? Do you think they will accuse you of the same thing Legend just did?"

"No. What Legend did was stupid. He wasn't looking for a wife. I'm simply choosing my bride, Colette. Now, if this woman that you speak of is what I've been looking for, then I will have my bride tonight."

"I think you should talk to your parents first before you do this. I don't want them to be upset with me for helping you break the covenant."

"They won't be upset with you, Colette. I won't tell them that you were the one that introduced me to her. Plus, if I don't like her, it would be a waste of time to tell them something I'm not sure of myself."

"I hope it goes well."

"It will. Don't worry."

"We're on our way," Colette said.

"I'll be at the bar, working, as usual. Bring her to me as soon as you get there."

"She is something special. You'll love her," Colette reassured me. "She likes confidence and you have *enough* of it for the whole world."

"You trying to call me conceited or something?"

"I'm not trying. I'm saying it." She laughed.

"Whatever."

"Yeah, okay, whatever. Wear that shit well 'cause this may be your only chance to win her over."

"I'll see you soon."

As soon as I hopped out of the taxi and my black leather Cabo Gancia Strap loafers hit the wet pavement, I felt a little anxiousness hit me. I took in a deep breath and exhaled. For decades, I'd searched high and low for a bride. That's not saying I wasn't close many times, but this time was going to be different.

"You good?" Onyx asked as soon as I made my way through the crowded line and up to the club's front door.

"I'm good," I replied, flashing him a quick smile.

When I entered into Club Vaisseau, the place was already starting to fill up with a host of the most beautiful women in the world. Loud house music was bumping. After scanning the club of some familiar faces, I went over to the bar. Legend and a new face were serving drinks.

"Who's this?" I asked Legend with a frown and hopped over the bar.

"This is our new girl…Soleil."

"Ah, *Bonsoir, Soleil.* I'm the youngest brother, Rain."

"*Bonsoir, Rain.* It's a pleasure to meet you."

"Ditto."

"I hear the ladies go crazy over your…um…" She cleared her throat as her eyes scanned over the way I looked. "…drinks. Would you agree?"

"I would," I replied assertively.

"Looks like I could learn a lot from you."

I winked at her, removed my shirt, and checked the bar to make sure we didn't need to stock anything else. We were good for the moment.

"Do you always bartend without a shirt?" she asked with her right eyebrow raised.

"He *always* bartends without a shirt," Legend replied before I could. "Charming bastard always tries to steal all of the women."

"That's a fabrication. He likes to bend the truth. Legend and Onyx take home just as many women, but Legend's days of frolicking and playing are over. He is officially off the market."

Legend rolled his eyes, slid a drink across the bar, and collected the money for it.

"Well, okay then," Soleil replied with a head nod.

I did a double-take when I spotted Colette and her friend at the entrance. I paused. Colette's friend was stunning, to the point where I wanted to make her mine right then without delay. Something about her fascinated me. The warmth of her blood illuminated her milk-chocolate skin and I wanted to taste her to see if she tasted like hot cocoa.

"Whoa," I said under my breath. That was all I could manage.

She and Colette made their way over to the bar, through the howling dance crowd of sweaty bodies pressed up against one another, ready to fuck. The naughty grin on her face made me aware of her arousal. I had to bite my own lower lip to stop myself from grinning. I wanted to know her name, so I could whisper it sweetly in her ear.

Colette's friend nodded her head to the music and began to sway her hips to the pulsating beat. The large blowing fans caused her wild, curly, jet-black hair to flow. She closed her eyes as if the pulse of the music electrified her.

When she opened them, her eyes immediately fell on Legend. He was spinning bottles, juggling glasses, and engaging every woman who crowded the bar around him. I could see that she was more than attracted to him. I could read her mind. She wanted to fuck him.

I chuckled to myself. My brothers caught a lot of women's attention. Therefore, I wasn't surprised about her attraction to him, but I couldn't help but feel a pinch of jealousy. I wanted to see what her reaction would be once she saw me. I wondered if I was her type.

As they approached the bar, they found a spot and secured it as their own. I made sure to disappear before she could see me. I appeared in front of them before they could put in their drink order. She saw *me*.

"What can I get you ladies?" I asked, leaning over the bar.

Her eyes became low and she couldn't turn away from my shirtless, sculpted body. She clutched her heart and made it obvious that she was into me.

I smiled on the inside while keeping a straight face.

Colette spoke up first, "Can you give us two shots of Vodka, *s'il vous plaît?*"

As I poured the liquor, Colette placed some money on the bar.

They started whispering to one another. I chose not to invade their privacy to hear what they were saying, though if I wanted to, I could hear every word. I slid the two shot glasses in front of them with well-practiced fluidity, not wasting a single drop on the glass-topped bar.

"Bottoms up!" the goddess yelled before downing the shot. Colette downed hers as well.

I placed two more shots in front of them before they were done.

"This one is on the house," I said with a wink before I made my way to the other end of the long bar.

I could feel her staring at me while I worked my magic. She was completely spellbound, fixated by the way I commanded her attention, and I hadn't hypnotized or transfixed her to do so. I didn't want to use any of my powers to persuade her. I wanted her to be attracted to me without manipulating her mind.

After fulfilling a few other drink requests, I was back in front of them. Legend covered me by taking over the end I'd abruptly abandoned.

"*Encore du Vodka, Mademoiselles?*" I asked with my left eyebrow raised.

"Give me one with cranberry juice this time," she replied.

"*Encore,*" Colette exclaimed as she shook her ass to the music.

As I poured more drinks to get them drunk, I admired *her* ebony skin, her eyes, her smile, high cheekbones, and cute button nose. Everything about her appearance was perfect to me. I couldn't keep my eyes off of her, and she couldn't keep her eyes off of me. Every time our eyes met, we smiled. Couldn't help it.

I licked my lips before asking, "Do you like what you see?"

"I do," she admitted quicker than I thought she would.

When she smiled wider, I knew I was going to have her.

"I've never seen you here before. Are you new to the city?" I questioned, though I already had the answer.

Colette told me her friend was from San Francisco, and studying abroad in Paris. Colette pretty much gave me all of the background info I needed, but I wanted to hear her friend tell me.

"I've been here for a few weeks. Maybe you can show me around some time."

"I would love to."

"Hopefully, you can show me more than the city…" she hinted.

I smiled broadly, staring at her before hopping from the other side of the bar swiftly. There was no bar between us anymore. I was so close to her, I could feel her heart beating rapidly up against my bare chest and I could smell her. She smelled so good.

"And your name is?" I asked.

"Essence."

"Essence. I like that… Come with me."

I didn't know if it was the liquor or if she was as horny as I was, but she let me take her hand while I led her through the club to the elevator. The elevator went up to the second floor. The second floor held rooms where we could do what we wanted to whom we wanted. Many times, we fulfilled plenty of fantasies, right there in those rooms.

"Where are we going?" she asked hesitantly.

"Do you trust me?"

She paused as if she had to think about it. "I trust you."

The golden elevator opened and we went up to the second floor. We went down a long dark hallway that was illuminated by red pulsating lights. I couldn't stop myself from pressing my body on hers so she could rest against the first door in the hallway. Soon, she would find out what kind of freakiness was going to happen behind it. The mere thought of fulfilling her wildest fantasies made my dick hard.

I leaned in closer to Essence before my tongue traced her lips. I hummed. "You taste too good." Both of my hands went into her curly hair. I moved her hair out of the way so I could place a kiss on her neck.

I made the door open up with my mind. I had that kind of power. I could move objects with telepathy. My hands were on the small of her back to catch her before she could fall from the door opening up so quickly.

She gasped, turning around to see that we were entering into a red velvet-covered bedroom with candles.

Once inside the room, I closed the doors with my mind.

"Pretty cool doors," she murmured while looking around the room.

A masked woman, erotically and scantily dressed, danced in each of the five narrow windows surrounding us. In addition to these peep shows, porn was playing on a high-definition flat-screen behind the round bed in the center of the room.

"Tell me something about you," Essence said, trying to break our silence.

I whirled her back around to me so I could put my lips to her ear. I whispered sweetly, "I'm the unspoken passion women secretly desire. You wonder about the mystery behind my eyes, don't you?"

"Yes," she whispered back.

"I am sex upright and poised. I am the lover you dream of."

I could feel her shudder underneath my touch, enthralled by every word that came from me.

Every inch of my skin crawled as I moved my hands all over her body. I was ready to see all of her, exposed, naked. But, that wasn't all I wanted to see. I wanted to get to know the beautiful woman for who she was. That really wouldn't matter; the woman she would become after the transformation would ultimately take over. I wanted to remember her the way she was, nonetheless.

"Rain…"

"Yes?"

Lifting her off her feet, I carried her to the plush bed covered in a golden silk comforter and laid her down gently.

"I want you to have me," she stated.

Placing my index finger over her lips, I hushed her from speaking. "Shhhh… Not another word."

Removing her halter top, jeans, laced panties and bra, I took off my black jeans. I slowly removed my boxers to reveal the rest of my skin. As my hands caressed her, I could feel her quivering. My lips went to her nipples and my tongue roamed.

"A storm is on its way," I uttered, before flicking my tongue back and forth. "Can't you feel it?"

While my fingers played around with her clit simultaneously, I slipped through her crevasses and found her soft wet spot, fingering her slowly.

Moving her hands to my dick, I could tell she was more than ready to feel me inside of her. She stroked me and I moaned. Guiding me to her sweet center, I inched my way inside of her. She gasped as I filled her up to capacity, skillfully, moving in and out of her.

The juices trickled between her legs and I kissed her lips, keeping at a steady pace. I didn't want to interrupt the flow. I moaned louder against her lips, feeling powerful with each pounding stroke, rhythm far from timid. Knowing exactly how I wanted to please her,

I had no problem helping her reach the purest form of ecstasy. I lifted one of her legs and rested it on my shoulder as I clutched her ass with both hands. Deeper, I went.

I could feel my fangs coming to the surface. As I stared down at her, I could tell she was mesmerized by the fire in her eyes. Suddenly, her body stiffened completely and her arms dropped limply to her sides.

I immobilized her. That was the best way to make her trapped inside of her own mind, so she wouldn't be able to scream if she was afraid of what I was revealing. I caressed the side of her face with my fingertips, turning her head slightly to the right.

Selfish thinking was something I needed to work on, but how could I pass on making this woman mine? I would deal with my family later. Essence was made for me. I felt that way. Colette knew it, too; that was why she'd brought her to me.

I placed my lips on her neck and her blood pumped through her veins against my cold lips. I quickly removed my lips from her skin because a part of me was too afraid of the outcome. What would I do if this plan backfired? I couldn't worry about that. One thing was for sure: I wanted Essence to love me and I wanted to love her. I kissed her neck softly again, this time opening my mouth to bite her. The first taste of her sweet warm blood caused me to moan instantly. I sucked. I sucked some more.

Her blood was delicious.

Essence started taking deep breaths. The bite made tears come to her eyes, yet she was moaning, so I moved in and out of her while I sucked. As soon as I stopped myself from drinking too much, I gazed at her while her blood oozed from the sides of my mouth.

I bit my own wrist and my blood dripped onto the floor. I put my bloody wrist up to her mouth so she could drink my blood. Her eyes were wide as she stared up at me in disbelief. Her chest heaved up and down while she breathed hard and she drank me.

"Relax," I said easily and calmly, keeping myself inside of her.

When I thrust my hips into her, I could feel her orgasm coming, so I rocked inside of her deeper, faster, and then harder. Her body went through this tremendous quake until she couldn't take it anymore.

Once she came, I sucked every bit of blood from her. She died in my arms. I kept my eyes on her and within minutes, her eyes opened back up. She moved her hands to her neck to feel the spot I'd bitten. My blood was healing her so quickly it was as if it had never taken place.

"Where's Colette?" she shrieked.

"She's one of us… She brought you to me."

"What does that mean?"

"It means that you are mine for an eternity."

"For an eternity?"

"Yes."

"Is that what you want from me?" she asked with a deep frown on her beautiful face.

"That's what I *need* from you."

I kissed her from her chin down to the center of her belly button. I spread her legs wider as I buried myself between her thighs to distract her from the pain. As she had another orgasm, her fangs emerged.

CHAPTER 5

AZURA

"So, how are things with your new bride, Legend?" I asked with a chuckle, while counting the money from the front door after we closed for the night.

"Azura…" Legend looked at me irritated as he loosened up his tie.

One thing about Legend was that he could outdress anyone. His fashion sense was dope and on another level, custom-made mostly. I would never spend the kind of money he did on clothes and I was a woman who loved clothes. His love for fashion showed in everything he put on. He did all of that flossing with his cash to impress women.

All of that was over now. I couldn't help but laugh on the inside that he'd decided to give up his whorish-ass ways for a woman he hardly even knew. What an idiot. I didn't believe for one second that he'd bit Chantal by accident.

"I'm taking it one day at a time," he answered.

"I must say, you're doing better than I thought you would. Having any urges to be in someone else's bed yet?"

"Nope," he replied and then shouted across the room, "Hey, Onyx, are there any more bottles of vodka upstairs? We're running low."

"We have plenty up there," Onyx replied as he walked over to the bar. "Hey, Azura, hook me up with Soleil."

I frowned as if he were crazy. "I don't think so."

"Aw, come on," Onyx answered.

"I'm so serious. No."

"Azura, please."

"Why can't any of you keep your dick in your pants and leave the staff alone? Mother and Father should make a rule that you can't go around sleeping with the help."

"That rule would constantly be broken, so they wouldn't dare." Legend laughed with Rain.

"Pay me and then I might hook you up," I stated.

"Come on, I'm your brother. A hookup never involves monetary rewards."

"On what planet? I refuse to hook your ass up for free... Plus, I don't even think she's checking for you like that...I think she has her eyes set on Rain."

"Rain?" Onyx scowled.

Rain shrugged and brandished that cocky smile of his.

All three of my brothers attracted different types of women and they didn't fight over chicks; there were plenty of women not to.

"That's my observation. Soleil couldn't keep her eyes off Rain all night."

"Well, shit, that's because Rain bartends shirtless. If I stood at the door with my shirt off and shit, she would be staring at me, too." Onyx smirked.

"You're such a hater," Rain said.

I laughed.

Onyx rolled his eyes.

Onyx wasn't as confident as Legend and Rain. He never had been. I think the long scar on the left side of his face made him insecure. The imperfection ran through his eyebrow to his cheekbone, but it didn't alter his appearance. It made his self-confidence a little lower.

Onyx begged, "Please do this for me. Soleil is so fine that I'll drink her bathwater."

"You would drink her dirty-ass bathwater?" Legend asked, scowling. "She's pretty, but you've lost your mind."

"I would and she has ass for days."

I loved these types of conversations with my brothers. I flipped my long hair off my shoulder and asked, "Onyx, if you had a choice between work and big-booty Soleil, which one would you choose?"

"Come on, Azura," Onyx answered. "You can't make me choose like that. That's not fair."

"It is fair. Our club is family owned and family comes first. Mother and Father don't stand for any foolishness and you know that."

"I respect our parents," Onyx replied. "But, Soleil might make me break all the rules. She's that fine."

Legend, Rain, and I laughed at him. I took the glasses out of the dishwasher and stacked them.

CHAPTER 6

ESSENCE

I fluttered my eyelashes and my eyes opened. I stared up at the ceiling before sitting up. I was back in the dorm, lying in my bed, with a massive hangover that threatened to keep me there. I tried to swallow, but my throat was so dry that my own saliva wasn't helping to keep it moist. I rubbed my neck and felt a thin necklace with some sort of charm. Where did it come from?

"Bonsoir," Colette sang as she entered our room with a brown paper bag of things from the store.

I frowned deeply, stared out of the open window into the night, and inhaled the smell of the dank air after a rainstorm. "It isn't morning? I thought it was morning. You mean to tell me it's still after dark. I must've partied excessively hard. I hardly remember a thing."

"You're still deliriously tired… You've slept a whole day."

"Are you kidding me?"

"No, not kidding."

"It's the strangest thing. I don't remember coming home and I feel like I've been sleeping forever. The last thing I remember is sitting at the bar drinking...and then…"

Colette came closer to me. *"What* and *who* do you remember?"

Thinking for a moment, I tried to recollect the night in the Red Light District and everything was a terrible blur. "…Nothing… and…nobody… Where did I get this necklace from?"

"Are you hungry? You should be starving by now. I can whip you up something to eat…chicken fettuccini, garlic bread, and a salad…"

The thought of cooked food made me nauseous instantly. "No," I replied quickly. "I'm starving, but I don't want that."

"What do you want?"

I held my head. "I feel so strange…"

"Here, lie back down," Colette instructed, coming to my bedside. She adjusted the pillow and I relaxed against it. "You need to rest."

She took a thermal coffee mug from her purse and opened it. Suddenly, a pungent smell engulfed my nostrils. Whatever was in the mug smelled delicious and my mouth began to water.

"What is that? It smells so good." I licked my dry lips, feeling myself grow anxious to drink what she had.

"Relax. I'm going to give you what you *need*."

Colette poured a red thickened liquid into an empty cup on the nightstand.

I tried to sit straight up to take the cup from her quickly, but she pushed me back down on the bed. "You have to drink this slowly, Mademoiselle."

"Okay, please give it to me already."

Colette guided the cup to my lips, slowly tilting the cup. The first taste of the warm liquid made me close my eyes. It was so good that I couldn't help myself as I drank faster and faster until it was all gone.

"Thank you. What is that? Is there any more?"

Colette smiled and replied, "Shhhh… Get some rest."

As if there was some sort of sleeping agent in the drink, I fell back into a deep sleep. Honey-brown eyes and a precedent grin welcomed me to the land of slumber.

CHAPTER 7

RAIN

At eight o'clock each night, my family prepared the club to open for business at ten. Azura counted the money in the registers, Onyx pulled the barstools down from the bar counters, Legend made sure all the light bulbs were working properly, and I couldn't focus. There was only one person on my mind... *Essence*...

I needed to see if her transition was going okay. I trusted Colette to look after her, but she hadn't called me as I'd instructed. I was growing impatient. I needed to see Essence. I'd never craved to feel a woman so much.

Azura tried to read my dazed expression, but I blocked her out of my head.

"We need some more vodka over here before we open and you over there daydreaming. What are you thinking about?"

"Nothing," I replied quickly.

Father and Mother walked through the front doors, locking them behind them.

"You just had to have her, didn't you?" Father stated with his nostrils flaring in anger.

I didn't respond.

"Rain, we always said you can have as many women as you desire in your bed, but why her?" Mother added with a hint of sadness and betrayal wrapped up in her voice.

Azura's, Onyx's, and Legend's ears perked up.

"What's going on?" Legend asked, moving his dreads over his shoulder.

"Nothing," I answered.

Why didn't they trust me? My judgment should've been enough for them to trust me.

"Your mortal is going through the transition right now, as we speak. That's far from nothing," Father responded.

"Tell me you didn't do that, Rain," Azura said.

I stared at my family, feeling as if I didn't have to explain why I'd chosen Essence to be the one for me. I wanted to share love with someone special, and she was that someone I wanted. I didn't see why that had anything to do with them.

"I did, but trust me, she's perfect."

Legend groaned.

Onyx looked worried as he said, "You could've discussed this with us before you went off and made that decision. Who is she?"

"Her name is Essence…"

"What do you know about this girl?" Mother questioned.

"She's a twenty-one-year-old student, studying here from San Francisco. As I said, she's perfect for me. I want to spend the rest of my life with her."

"What if her family worries about her?"

"She doesn't have any family. She's an orphan that was raised by numerous foster families."

"You have a purpose that even you don't fully understand yet," Father yelled, slamming his fist on top of the bar and causing the top to slightly crack. "You can't just up and decide who you want to be your bride. Mortals have no understanding to this life. Do you think she will accept this and be in love with you?"

"There's no doubt in my mind."

"How stupid can you really be? Sometimes, I wonder if you even understand what you were chosen to become, who you're destined to be. The Divination is not to be taken so lightly. All of you take it too lightly."

"I'm beginning to think the Divination is a bunch of bullshit," I said underneath my breath.

Father stared at me with such a fire in his eyes that they turned red. "Don't you dare say that again."

"How many more years will it be before this great thing is supposed to happen to me? We've roamed this earth for far too many centuries. It's time for me to take matters into my own hands and live my life the way I want to."

Before Father could act out violently, Mother interjected, "Love from a woman seems to be what you're missing. We shouldn't have to tell you whom to love. We aren't like other vampires. We have a mission to carry out. Though, we don't know when we will be able to, we still have to do things a certain way."

"How long will it be?"

"I'm not sure… Look, all we ask is that you talk to us before doing what you did. Now, all we can do is sit back and see what side she'll join," Mother said.

"Colette is making sure she chooses right."

"Look how long it took Colette to realize which side is right. If this transition goes the wrong way, you can predict what's going to happen next. I think you should be there, at her side, to make sure. Don't leave your mess up to Colette. So, when this goes bad, you'll only have yourself to blame," Father growled through gritted teeth.

"You think I should go to her?"

"You should go right now!" Father commanded.

CHAPTER 8

ESSENCE

When I woke up, familiar honey-brown eyes were staring down at me. The memory of him came crashing down into my memory bank. He wasn't simply a dream. He was real. He was standing before me. I panicked, but found I couldn't move away from him. The man they called Rain was here. God, he was so gorgeous, all I could do was stare at his beautiful dark skin. As he bent down over me, I felt a blast of pure lust. My center was hot, wet, and ready for him to take me again.

"I thought you were a figment of my imagination," I uttered, feeling my nipples become aroused without him even touching me. "Or simply a wonderful dream that I never want to wake up from."

His voice was deep and sexy as he replied, "I'm real. I came to make sure you're okay. How are you feeling? What are your thoughts?"

"I'm okay... Did you give this necklace to me?"

He bent his head down, lowered his thick lips to touch my neck, and I felt him inhale me. "It's my gift to you. Do you like it?"

"It's very pretty. Solid gold?" I asked, feeling very confused and dizzy all of a sudden.

"Twenty-four karats. Keep it around your neck or hide it in a safe spot. It's something my birth mother gave to me at a young age. It matches mine."

He flashed his chain. The two pieces looked like they would fit together like a puzzle if linked.

"It's beautiful. Thank you."

"You're welcome."

"Why did you bite me?"

"I must admit that what I did to you was very selfish, and I'm not sure how you're going to feel, but I want you to be mine for eternity. Can you handle that?"

I smiled up at him because the thought seemed romantic. I touched his cold face with the palm of my hand, lifted myself up toward him, and captured a kiss from his lips. He lowered his kiss down to my neck, over the spot he'd tenderly bitten, and let his tongue roam freely.

Baring my new fangs, I let out a hiss, feeling this crazed uncontrollable need for his sex.

Rain took ahold of my jaw making my mouth open up for him so he could take a good look. "You, my lady, are a vampire."

The thought suddenly scared me. If I was a vampire, that meant I was no longer alive. What would people think? Whom could I tell? How would I tell my friends? Feeling this incredible strength inside of me, I pushed him off of me. He flew across the room and crashed onto the floor. Tears wanted to fall from my face.

"What am I going to do now? Am I going to continue to sleep the day away and awake every night feeling this need for blood and sex?"

"That's why I'm here to help you," he replied, standing on his two feet. "There's a whole new life ahead of you and you can't go back to doing things the way you did them before. If you're not careful, you'll kill anyone for blood and your insatiable desire for sex will become uncontrollable."

"Why'd you choose me?"

He was back by the bedside in the blink of an eye. "You're so beautiful. I had to have you."

My hunger was back. My stomach pangs confirmed that I wanted to eat. "I'm so hungry. Where's Colette? I need something to eat."

"Colette won't be helping you anymore. I'm going to make sure you get everything you need."

"Okay… Do you have anything to eat?"

CHAPTER 9

RAIN

Bringing her back to Club Vaisseau in the middle of her transition was dangerous, but she needed blood. I hoped her thirst wouldn't allow her to kill to get it. Once she had her first kill, the thrill from it would be too powerful, and she would no longer be one of us. One of the dark broods would have no problem taking in another scavenger.

We had spare blood from blood givers. They gave their blood willingly to keep us alive in case of emergencies. Every night, in a small room inside the club, we collected blood and it was smooth and easy. We hunted normally, but this blood was for our emergencies only.

If she didn't get enough as needed, she would die. I could've taken her on her first hunt, but since it was excessively early to be exposed, I had to go into our emergency reserve. I wanted her to realize what was happening gradually. The smell of humans would possibly send her over the edge, and her strength at this tender moment would be too strong for me to control, but I took the risk anyway.

As I escorted her through the back of the club around midnight, I made sure she wouldn't come into contact with any humans. At that hour, the blood drive was usually over, giving us more than enough to get us through to the next night.

As I expected, no one was in the room. I sat Essence down in a chair as her head rolled around. She was ready to get to sleep, but her hunger pangs wouldn't let her. If I didn't hurry, she was going to bolt out of the room at lightning speed and kill the first human she met.

I opened the warmer and got out an airtight thermal. As soon as the container was opened, she could smell it. She snatched it from me and drank it quickly. Suddenly, she calmed down. Wiping the excess blood from her mouth, she stared at me.

"Better?" I asked.

"I'm better now."

"Good." Worry fled from me. I could see the calm in her eyes. She was going to be fine.

"What's your real name, Rain?"

"I remember being called Eric, early on in my life. I was told that I'm not supposed to have many memories from my life before I changed, but for some reason, I remember a lot of it."

"You have a woman or a wife at home?" She rose up from the chair and floated toward me.

I took both of her hands in mine and lowered her feet to the ground.

"I'm married...to you."

Essence shook her head slowly. "No, you're not. Where's your wife and don't lie this time?"

"I just told you. I'm now married to you."

She laughed hysterically, as if what I'd said was too funny.

"It's not a joke. This is the way it works, here, in Pigalle Palace."

She leaned even closer to me and whispered in my ear, "You're one of the sexiest men I've ever laid eyes on. Your smooth skin, your dark eyes, and your incredible smile drives me wild. Can you really be all mines?"

"Yes, I'm all yours."

Her eyes lit up with fascination. "It's that simple, huh?"

"It's that simple."

She stared into my mouth as if she wanted to devour me. "When can we consummate our marriage?"

"We've already done that, but there's plenty more where that came from."

Essence moaned and wrapped her arms around my neck. "I hope you know what you created here."

"I know what I'm doing."

"Confident…I like. What are we going to do now? Stay in this tiny little room for the rest of the night?"

"You're going back to your dorm to get some rest because you need it."

"I think you should come with me. That sounds better, doesn't it?"

"I'm going to take you home, but I have to leave you because I'm working tonight. As soon as I'm off work, I'll be right there with you, sweetheart."

"Maybe you shouldn't work tonight."

"No can do."

She groaned.

"Listen, I promise to be there as soon as I'm off. I have to be here tonight."

"Aw, too bad because I'm so ready to have you all night long. This good pussy needs you."

The words *good pussy* made my dick harder than a military tank. I knew how good her pussy truly was. I picked her up and laid her on top of the table. In a flash, I had her pants off.

"Well, it looks like we're going to have to take care of that before I take you home," I uttered against her lips.

She wrapped her legs around my waist and moaned. Deep inside of her, I thrust, back and forth, causing the table to rock with us. She felt better than the last time I was inside of her. This was going to be quick. I felt it. Our sex felt too good to stop. At that moment, I wasn't worried one bit about anyone walking in on us. We were going to keep rocking until we both could no longer take it.

CHAPTER 10

LEGEND

"Legend," Chantal called from the hallway.

My wife was standing in front of a tall body-length mirror. Her hair was in big loose curls, neatly in place, and her lips were looking like fresh fruit, mouthwatering and succulent. Once she completed her transformation, she was truly a foxy woman. Even though her beauty had me feeling compounded, I couldn't help but see that she noticed she didn't have a reflection.

"What's the matter, Chantal?"

"This is crazy. I thought I would be able to see my reflection, but…"

"Your reflection is something you will never see again, so get used to it. I thought I got rid of all the mirrors in here…"

"I bought this one."

"Oh, I see."

I didn't understand where her mind was. If she couldn't see her reflection while at the store, why would she buy the mirror? Did she think it would magically appear once she got home?

"My best friend, Jade, has been looking for me. I don't know how to explain any of this. Will you help me?"

"How much longer will she be in town?"

"We were supposed to be leaving in two days. I don't know how she's going to react."

"You could always not say anything."

"She will think I've been kidnapped or something. I don't want her to worry."

I pulled back my dreads into a ponytail. "Well, then, you're going to have to make a decision. Either you can be a missing person or you can tell her the truth. The risk of any of those things is huge, but it's up to you."

She thought for a little bit before she said, "I noticed that I'm much stronger than I used to be. I lifted the whole bed this morning by accident. I was looking for my shoe."

"You'll start noticing a bunch of new things about yourself."

"Come here," she said.

I invaded her personal space and she pulled me against her. She started rubbing, creating warmth against my jeans, until she reached my crotch. She bit on her lower lip.

"I might have to take your ass in this bedroom if you keep it up," I said.

She giggled. "Seems like you bring the freak out in me. I can't help myself when I'm around. I feel this fiery passion all the time. It's like I crave to feel you inside of me every second of the day." She placed her breath on my neck before she kissed me. She began sucking on my neck. I felt her fangs graze me.

"Hey, be careful there. You've never bit anyone before and I don't want you testing it out on me."

Her bright eyes turned sad suddenly. I never allowed myself to feel any remorse about things I had done in the past. For some reason, my conscience was getting to me.

"I'm sorry for doing this to you," I apologized.

She shrugged slightly. "I wanted you to."

Her nonchalant attitude stirred my curiosity. "I need to know more about you. People usually learn these things before getting married. Where are you from?"

"Chicago."

"Chi-town. What brought you to Paris?"

"All my life I wanted to come to Paris. It was supposed to be the dream vacation."

"Is it not the dream vacation you hoped for? Seems to me you got what you came here for."

"I never actually believed in vampires until I came to the Red Light District. I've always heard about them. Once I got here, I had to see one in person."

"How come you weren't afraid of me?"

"The vampire's story has always intrigued me... Were you born a vampire?"

"No, we weren't born vampires. We were born with vampire blood. Our birth father was a vampire when he met our birth mother. She was...human." My voice trailed off. I rarely talked about our birth parents because it was hard for me to remember anything about them. We were so young when they were murdered. "The mother and father that you know aren't our real parents. They are our godparents, but they raised us because our parents were murdered. Being half-blooded only leads to death, so they trans-formed us."

"Where were you born?"

"My siblings and I were born in New Orleans. It became too dangerous for us, so we found a safe haven, here, in Paris with other vampires."

She played with my fingers. Mushy wasn't me, but for some reason I didn't object to her affection. "You have smooth hands. I like a man with smooth hands."

I didn't know anyone could make me feel the way she did.

"You should shower with me before I leave," I suggested.

"Ooooh, that sounds good."

She followed me to the bathroom. I turned on the shower and brought her body to mine as I caressed her.

"So, this is what it's like to be married to Legend."

"What does it feel like?"

"Feels perfect."

"Can I ask you something?"

"Sure…"

"Has a woman ever asked you to change her before?"

"I don't make it habit to lay with mortals. I tend to sleep with vampires only. I don't tell mortals too much. Curious mortals usually end up dead."

"Have you ever been in love before? I'm not talking about lust either. I'm talking about serious love."

"I've never ever been in love. Honestly, I've never wanted to be in love. I'm…or I should say I *was* a ladies' man."

There was so much mounted heat between us that I was ready to fuck her senseless. Chantal got out of my arms and adjusted the shower water to a nice temperature for the both of us.

"Legend, I'm sure a lot of women come in and out of your life. You have the charisma to charm the panties off any woman you want… Whether you chose me by accident or not, I'm here and it feels like we were meant to be. I don't believe in accidents. I believe in fate. This feels like fate."

"So, you think this is our destiny?"

Standing in her black see-through bra and panties, she removed her top. "Yes…and now, I'm waiting for you to accept that."

She put her arms around my neck and gazed into my eyes. Chantal seemed as if she was exactly the woman to change me for the better. I put my hand in the water. It was too hot, so I adjusted the knob again.

"I've never met a woman like you before."

She took off the rest of her underwear seductively. After pinning up her hair, she stepped into the water. "Are you going to get undressed and get in here? This was all your idea."

"I was waiting for you to undress me first."

"Oh, I'm sorry. I can still undress you."

"That's okay. I'll undress myself for you. You can do it next time."

I removed all of my clothes quickly and joined her inside of the steam unit. As soon as I was in, our lips met immediately. "Chantal," I whispered against her.

"Yeah?" she whispered back.

"I'm happy that you're with me."

"Only say it if you truly mean it," she replied.

"I mean it. I am falling in love with you."

"You don't mean that, Legend, or do you?"

"I mean it."

All kind of weird emotions poured from within me, yet I wasn't afraid to express myself.

While I washed her with the jojoba oil soap, I sucked the back of her neck, leaving a red passion mark on her light skin. She turned to face me. Taking the sponge from my hands, she washed my body and ran her fingers all over me.

I got on my knees, positioning myself between her legs. My dreads were getting wet, but I didn't care.

She moaned lowly. "You know what happened last time you were down there?"

"I promise not to bite this time."

I licked along her inner thigh, spreading her legs wider before blowing lightly on her clit. Her hands gripped my head as I made circles with my tongue on top of her pearl tongue. With each stroke of my tongue, her breathing increased. She rested her long legs on my shoulders. I sucked her clit, rolling my tongue skillfully.

She had my dreads in both fists as she grinded against my face. She gasped, "What are you trying to do to me, Legend?"

"What you want me to do to you now, Chantal?" I asked, rising to my feet.

She took ahold of me and guided me inside of her. Once inside, I thrust my hips into her.

"Oooooh, Chantal."

"I like the way you say my name." She moaned.

I loved watching her sex face as her walls clenched me tighter.

"Whose pussy is this?" I asked.

"Yours."

"Who am I?"

She panted as she moaned and exclaimed, "Legend!"

CHAPTER 11

RAIN

I remember the New Orleans hurricane of 1915. It was the day that I became immortal. The storm began on the night of September 28 and reared its ugly head by the date of my birth, September 29. It became extra tropical at 7 a.m. and we had winds of 130 miles per hour by nightfall.

I paced back and forth in the shadows of the darkened underground room. I could hear the horrible gusts of wind rattling and shaking the whole house. All windows, doors, and hurricane shutters were closed and boarded up with plywood, but it seemed like our roof was about to be ripped off. Our power had already gone out, so candles were the only light we had.

I wasn't afraid of the hurricane. I was terrified of something much greater.

I was old enough to grasp the concept of what I was to become, but I feared this night. I wanted so desperately to change the hands of time so I wouldn't have to go through with it. There was nothing I could do. Pacing my bedroom for a while longer, wearing nothing but underwear beneath a gray robe, my own questions refused to let me be idle.

Truthfully, I had no other choice. What I was about to become was irreversible; ultimately my destiny. My siblings had to go through it and it had saved their lives. It was my turn.

After taking a few long deep breaths, I stared at myself in the mirror because it would be the very last time I would ever see my reflection again. That alone made me wish that I were dead instead.

A single knock on my bedroom door jarred me out of my bottomless thoughts. "Come in," I said.

My godfather entered the bedroom. We called him Father. He said, "It's time."

I took a very deep breath, exhaled, and then followed him down the candlelit hallway of our home. My rapidly beating heart pounded and drummed faster the closer with each step. I clutched the necklace my birth mother had given me before she and my birth father were murdered. I'd had it in my possession since I was five years old. I never lost it.

My godmother, Serene, whom had been in our lives since then, gently closed the door behind us. We called her Mother. Wearing full hooded black cloaks, Legend and Onyx held candles with both hands.

"Eric," Azura said, taking a whiff of my neck. "Tonight is a very special night for all of us. You'll be the only one to touch the sun and you'll be able to reign as King one day. The Divination can now hold true."

She gently placed a kiss on the side of my face. It was soft and gentle, a sisterly kiss. I stared at her trapped youth for a moment before swallowing the hard lump that was forming in my throat. The fact that I, too, would never age, grow old, or die was too much for me to fathom. To roam the earth for eternity was something no human could do.

I bowed gracefully at Azura.

"Remove your robe," Mother ordered sternly.

I did what I was told. As the robe fell to my feet, Azura took my hand into hers. She led me to the bed where I lay down. Legend and Onyx placed the candles by the bedside. Legend started to tie my right hand first and then right foot to the edges of each bedpost with strong ropes that couldn't be broken. Onyx did the same to my left arm and leg. My breathing became more intense.

Father came to the end of the bed and asked, "Is he secure?"

"Yes," Legend and Onyx replied in unison checking the ropes.

"Why do I have to be restrained?" I questioned, feeling the pit of my stomach turn flips.

"The ropes are there to protect you. Your body is going to go through a series of unexplainable pains. It's going to feel like torture. You're going to have an insatiable thirst for human blood and want to kill to quench that thirst. We don't believe in killing to quench our thirsts and wouldn't want you to harm anyone."

Father nodded his head at Mother.

"Are you sure this is the only way?" I asked for the last time with tears filling my eyes.

"The only way!" Mother almost yelled. "You ask too many damned questions."

The room fell silent. The only sound we could hear was the hurricane's roar against the house.

Azura removed her cloak, came to the side of the bed, and stared down at me for a moment. Her eyes turned red as soon as my eyes locked with hers. I was mesmerized by the fire in them. She caressed the side of my face with her fingers and turned my head slightly to the right.

She cut her wrist with a dagger that was on the table. Her blood oozed out into a goblet. She added a small vile of poison—poison that would make my heart stop. She brought the cup to my lips for me to drink. I drank it quickly.

As soon as I lay back down, I felt this unbearable pain escalate from the top of my head to my toes.

Azura covered her eyes. To see me in such pain brought her to tears. Legend comforted her by wrapping his big strong arms around her.

I started mildly shaking before going into a wild convulsion I couldn't control. Though I was bound, it seemed as if I was going to break the ropes. My wrists and ankles bled from fighting to get free. I screamed and howled, "Please…stop this!"

"I can't watch," Azura said, fleeing the room, and sobbing loudly. She could no longer take my agonized screams.

Mother closed the door behind her. For a few more minutes, they watched over me until I stopped shaking. They all finally left the room except for Mother.

"Your mother would be so proud at this moment. She loved you very much."

I heard her talking to me, but I was losing consciousness.

She smiled down at me before placing a sweet kiss on my forehead. I felt chills as all warmth started leaving my body. My heart had stopped beating, but my eyes were still open. Seconds later, I blinked.

The hurricane of September 29, 1915, with its great rainfall, high winds and high tides, was by far the worst storm New Orleans had seen. Seemed like at that moment, the storm was at its peak.

"From now on, you shall be called Rain."

I remember it like it was yesterday. A memory that hadn't been erased. I had all of my memories unlike my siblings. They remembered very little about our childhood and they had no memory of our birth parents at all.

As the years rolled by, I had only been in love a few times and one of them was a mortal. I didn't want to change her because I didn't want her to live with this curse—to roam the Earth forever without being able to see your own reflection. That ability was something I wished I could get back.

This time, Essence was going to be the one I was going to spend eternity with because she was perfect for me.

Colette wanted to throw Essence a birthday party at Vaisseau to celebrate her twenty-second birthday. Since I'd changed her weeks earlier, I agreed it would be a good idea for her to enjoy her last birthday party.

It was a big event fit for a princess. I worked the bar with Legend and Soleil. Onyx was at the door and Azura collected money as usual.

People were swarming all over the place.

Essence stood at the bar. She looked sexy as fuck in that dress that clung to her body like Saran Wrap. My eyes traveled to the much cleavage she revealed and then down to her legs. I came to her side of the bar to fix her a drink.

"Rain, I'm so happy to be celebrating my twenty-second birthday."

"I'm happy for you. You should celebrate your birthday every year. That is something we don't do at all."

"You don't celebrate yours?"

"No, we don't celebrate. That's by choice. Birthdays are a reminder of what was… After so many birthdays, it's pointless. For you, this is still so fresh. You should celebrate as much as you need to."

Suddenly, there were tears in her eyes. "This has all been driving me crazy, Rain…"

"I know. In time, things will start fading and certain feelings about things will go away."

I reached out to touch her hand, but she moved it before I could. I frowned a little.

"I've decided to stay with Colette for a little while," she stated.

"For the night?"

"No, for a little while. To get my head clear."

"I don't understand."

"I'll see you later…" She hopped off the stool and walked toward the other direction to the dance floor.

Legend put his hand on my shoulder. "She'll come around, bro."

Soleil interrupted before I could answer, "You better hope she doesn't sleep with another man. Once she does that, your bond will be broken and the marriage will be over."

That was a part of the vampire marriage covenant.

"She's confused right now," I said, while I watched her grind with some other man on the dance floor. I gritted my teeth and fixed a drink for myself.

A stunning, dark-skinned woman maneuvered and found a spot at the bar. Skin was exposed everywhere in her skimpy gold dress that hugged her body just right and showed off every asset. She flung her long hair over her shoulder as she bit on her lower lip, and used her index finger to lure Legend in. When he didn't budge, she leaned across the bar toward him.

"Legend?" she asked him in the sexiest voice.

"That's me."

"Come upstairs with me," she said with bright eyes.

He turned away from her and focused on the dance floor.

"Hey, are you looking to have a good time? I can give you the best time of your life."

"No, thanks."

Legend never turned down a model chick that rated a ten on the scale. Ever since Chantal had become his wife, he had been changing for the better.

"Well, if you ever need anyone, here's my number." She tried to slip a card into the palm of his hand, but he didn't take it.

She placed it on the bar and walked away. Her ass looked as juicy as a ripe mango underneath that short dress.

"Who was that?" Onyx asked.

"I don't know," Legend replied with a shrug. "Have you seen Chantal?"

"She's in the lounge," I said.

I looked to see if I could see Essence. She had disappeared into the crowd. I took in a deep breath and returned to the bar. I was hoping to see her one more time before the night was over, but that didn't happen.

CHAPTER 12

LEGEND

She astounded me in her red elegant, short, thin-strapped dress while she sat on a red couch in the lounge. A stylist hooked up her hair. I gifted the diamond earrings that were dangling from each earlobe.

"Did I already tell you that you look amazing tonight," I complimented.

"Yes, Legend, but I'll hear it again. Thanks to you." Chantal blushed while looking around the club. "This is a really nice turnout for Essence's birthday."

"It really is. I'm enjoying myself." I placed a kiss on her exposed shoulder.

She backed away a little. "Before me, did you treat all your women like this?"

"All my women?"

"Yeah… I'm sure all your women were beating down your door before you bit me."

"Chantal, I never made any promises to anyone. I never broke any hearts. I never made any kind of commitment, so I didn't take care of any of them the way I take care of you."

"Were you a womanizer?"

"Why are you asking?"

"A few women in here keep staring at me and I even heard a few talking about how they had you and still can have you. You're pretty popular around here."

"I used to be a wild boy. Let's not forget how I got you back to my place."

She shook her head. "My jealousy is out of control tonight."

"Everything is heightened. Any emotion you feel will be so intense this way. I have something for you."

I took a ring out of my pocket. Even though we were already married, I hadn't given her a ring yet.

"What's that?"

"A wedding ring..."

She shook her head in disbelief as I slid the ring on her finger. Tears threatened to ruin her makeup and stain her face.

"Oh, this ring is amazing." She had that hypnotized look in her eyes.

At first, I thought it was going to be too much for her. The six-carat diamond ring was far from simple.

"Chantal, you're my wife and as my wife, I want you to wear it."

A big smile came across her face. "Are you ready to go home right now? I'm ready to get you home so we can make love all night long."

"That sounds like a plan, but don't worry 'cause I got something in store for you as soon as we get home."

She hugged me. I kissed her long and hard in front of every woman in the building. The looks on their faces were priceless. Chantal was all smiles after that.

CHAPTER 13

ONYX

Helping out with the family business was something that I loved and we always had a blast working together. Azura could have as many men as she wanted and we could have any woman we desired. Since Rain and Legend were officially off the market, I could do anything with any woman. Club Vaisseau was exactly what we needed to feed our large appetite for sex, but lately I'd had my eyes on one woman only, Soleil.

I shut down the register at the bar and began organizing the receipts on the bar.

Azura took her private party upstairs leaving Soleil and me alone. Finally, I thought to myself, this was the perfect time to flirt with her. While I was thinking of what to say, she beat me to the punch.

"Are you heading out in a bit?"

"Yeah. You on your way out, too?" I asked.

"As a matter of fact, I am."

She put the wet rag away and I watched.

I believed she came to work to impress me, wearing the extra-sweet-smelling perfumes. Her wild golden locks were like tiny, long spiraled curls in the form of an afro. Every time she was near me, I had to bite on my lower lip to contain the attraction I felt. She was that sexy. Her gold curly hair, flawless natural makeup, perfect dimpled grin, and brown eyes had me feeling like I was in love.

"Would you like to share a cab?"

She didn't hesitate. "Sounds good to me. Let's go, handsome."

After shutting off the lights, and locking the door, we walked down the alley out to the street to catch a cab. One was pulling up at the right time and we hopped in. We were going to two different locations, but I didn't mind riding with her. I wanted to stay in her presence for as long as I could. I couldn't keep my eyes off the way her breasts were nearly popping out of her corset.

"Why do you keep staring at my boobs?" she asked.

I chuckled. I was busted. "You look very nice tonight... You look very nice every night."

"Thank you. You're not so bad yourself. How come you're single?"

"Why don't you have a man?"

"What makes you think I don't have a man?"

"What makes you think I'm single?"

"Azura told me. What makes you think I'm available?" she asked.

"If you had a man, I don't think you would've let me share this cab with you tonight."

"This cab ride doesn't mean anything, Onyx. My man could be at home waiting for me."

"But, he's not 'cause there is no man at home waiting for you." I bit on my lower lip and then said, "You're gorgeous."

She laughed to blow me off and turned her eyes to the window. "You're such a bad boy."

"Am I a bad boy?"

"I know more than you think, Onyx. You hadn't always been the good son. That scar on your face tells a rough story... How'd it happen?"

"Long story. One day, I'll share it."

She stared at me sincerely. "The scar is...erotic."

"Erotic? When I look at it, I tend to block out how it got there."

"Yes...erotic..."

"Are you flirting with me?"

She giggled. "No."

"No?" I raised my eyebrows.

"Are you flirting with me?" She turned my question around on me.

"Maybe a little...I just might be."

Her eyes sparkled whenever the taxi passed underneath a street lamp. "I have a confession... There are times when I daydream of fucking someone right on top of that bar inside of the club."

"You serious?"

"There's something about Club Vaisseau that's so sexy to me." She played with her hair, twirling it around her index finger.

"Club Vaisseau exudes sex."

"Yes. I can see why there is a need for the *special* rooms upstairs."

"You should check them out one day. Who is this someone you fuck on the bar in your daydreams?"

"He never has a face, but the bar is clear as day."

"Hmmm, are there people surrounding the bar watching?"

"No, it's me and him, alone..."

"Are you sure it isn't me you're fucking on the bar?"

She stared at me with a gleam of desire in her eyes. She laughed it off. "You think I dream about fucking you on the bar? What part of Paris do you stay?" she asked, diverting my question.

"The north hill of Paris."

"Ah, Montmartre."

"Yes. You?"

"I live near Bordeaux."

"That's quite a ways away."

She hummed and replied, "I know."

"Will I beat the sun home?"

"You should be okay."

"What if I'm not?" I asked. "Will you let me stay at your place?"

My eyes gazed at the way she ran her fingers through her curly hair. The mounted sexual tension between us was peaking. I could feel it.

"I don't think so." Her words were direct, but her smile told me different.

"I think you're scared to tell me that I'm that *someone* you fuck on top of the bar."

"You better be glad we're not at work right now," she teased. "You could get in trouble for sexual harassment." Her dimpled grin was winning me over by the second.

"Sexual harassment? This is your daydream, remember?"

"True, but I'm not harassing you. I was sharing my dream."

"Are you seeing anyone?" I asked anyway as if I didn't know.

"I'm interested in someone."

"Could this someone be me?"

"Maybe."

I watched how her tongue licked the inside of her lips slowly and I was digging everything about the golden-haired goddess. I wanted to learn all there was about her.

"Tell me more about this fantasy."

"No..." She laughed.

"I want to hear more... in detail."

Her dimples deepened as her smile expanded. "No."

She made flirting fun. I knew my boundaries. We got to know one another in the backseat of the cab, laughed, and left open-ended questions so we could flirt some more.

The cab pulled up to her spot sooner than I wanted him to.

She asked the cab driver, "How much?"

"I'll cover it once I'm dropped off," I interrupted.

"Thank you. See you tomorrow."

She smiled at me before hopping out of the cab. I watched her walk up the stairs of the building to her nice apartment home.

"Hey, don't drive off until she's inside."

The cab driver nodded his head and did what I instructed. Once she was inside, he pulled away from the curb. I smiled to myself, feeling more determined to get her to be mine.

The next evening, I went to work an hour early, hoping that Soleil would be there early as well. As the cab pulled up, I saw Soleil standing at the front door.

"Is anyone here yet?" I asked.

"No."

I was hoping we would be alone. My insides jumped for joy.

"What are you doing here?" I lifted my eyebrow, hoping she would tell me she was thinking about me when she decided to come to work early.

"I had a feeling that you would be here. Plus, I want to practice making this new drink I want to feature tonight."

Soleil was wearing a short black dress and I gazed at her legs. A naughty smile came to my face as I unlocked the door. I turned on the lights.

She went and sat right on top of the bar and spread her legs. That's when I noticed she wasn't wearing any underwear. As I stood there, watching in awe, she pulled me by my shirt.

"I had that dream again..."

"It was me, wasn't it?"

She nodded and kissed me hard. I hiked up her dress and moved my hand to feel her clit. She was soaking wet. She unbuttoned my pants and placed her hands in my boxer briefs. She smiled widely and moaned. I pushed her on her back on top of the bar, lifting her legs up. Without shame or guilt, our pure unadulterated X-rated sex was taboo.

I flipped her around, bent her over. While her hands gripped the edge of the bar, I fucked her hard from behind. Each thrust sent her into a frenzy while she panted.

As I climaxed, I kept my eyes closed shut. I had to make it a quickie because someone would be walking in the door any moment. I shuddered when I came.

"Wow," she said, standing up straight. "You want to come to my place after work? We can share another cab."

"It would be my pleasure."

She kissed me as if I were too irresistible. I moved my kisses to her neck, pinning her back up against the bar.

"You better quit before we be at this all night," she said. She shoved her tongue in my mouth one last time.

I moaned, feeling the passion level go back up. "That wouldn't be a problem, would it?"

She laughed devilishly before getting out of my reach. "We'll have more time later."

I fixed my clothes and she straightened herself out before sauntering to the bathroom.

It was hard to concentrate throughout the rest of the night without looking at Soleil. Every time I stared at her while she worked the bar, I felt myself rise. Whenever no one else was looking, she lipped, "Fuck me."

By the time our work shift ended, we couldn't keep our hands off one another. As soon as we were in her apartment, we were ready for round two. I found myself unable to speak as she grabbed ahold of me roughly, pulling me into her bedroom. She led me into her love den, kissing me the whole way, taking off my clothes.

We collapsed on her bed.

"Wait, wait, wait," she said, halting, cutting my kisses off. "I don't want you to think that I do this all the time."

"I don't think that."

"What you think then?" she asked, kissing me again.

"I'm not thinking..."

More kisses until we were completely naked.

Her phone rang.

I stopped, but she kept kissing my body.

"Your phone..." I said.

She shook her head no. We were doing something that was more important and more urgent than whoever was calling.

Sex with Soleil became wild. We knocked over lamps, broke vases, and pictures fell from the walls. Her headboard sounded like it wanted to go through the wall every time I thrust into her. Hot. Sweaty. Her golden hair in my hands. Intense. In the kitchen. Biting. Nails in my back. On the living room floor. Digging. Felt good. Too good. Couldn't stop. Back to the bed. Moaning. Screaming. Orgasms.

CHAPTER 14

RAIN

With Essence avoiding me for weeks as if I was some type of black plague, I was doing all I could to stop myself from going crazy. She had been staying in her dorm with Colette and hadn't talked to me since her birthday. I missed her, so I sent her different flowers every day with sweet notes to show I was thinking of her. There were so many types of exotic flowers. I made sure I sent ones she never heard of.

I decided to give her another call, hoping she would pick up this time.

She answered, "Hello."

"Hey… How are you? I haven't heard from you in a while."

"I know… Actually, I need to see you. Can I see you now?"

"Yes. Do you need me to come over there?"

"No. I'll be on my way to your place."

The sound of her voice made me worried. "Is everything all right?"

"Everything will be okay. Do you think we can go somewhere?"

"Where do you want to go?"

"I've always wanted to go to the Palace of Versailles. It was on my list of sites to see when I came to study abroad. Will you come with me?"

"Tonight?"

"Yes, tonight."

"As long as we're back before I have to work."

"You always have to work. Don't you get any time off?"

"What do I need to take time off for?"

"I think it's time for you to take a break."

I closed my eyes and inhaled before I exhaled. She was asking me to disappear or call in when my parents needed us to help run the club. It kept us busy and out of trouble. If someone was attacked by a vampire, our parents knew it wasn't one of us, but if taking time off meant winning her over, I was going to have to do that. "What time are you going to be here?"

"I'm waiting on Colette to get here so I can leave. Her class will be over in another half an hour."

"All right. Are you going to spend the night with me?"

"I don't know."

I rubbed my face, feeling frustrated. I was ready for her to come home.

"Essence…"

She cut me off. "Thanks for the flowers. I've been keeping to myself lately."

"Look, I understand that you're upset with me. I took away your choice. I was selfish. Yes, I can admit that. I wanted you from the moment I laid eyes on you. Am I not attractive to you anymore?"

"Yes, baby, you're attractive. I was looking for a great time that night. I don't know if I can deal with you taking my life away from me… But, I'm trying my absolute best to cope with the new me. Look, I'll see you soon. We'll talk then, okay?"

"All right."

She hung up.

I was going to have to call Azura to tell her I wasn't going to be able to work. Azura wasn't answering her phone, so I called Legend. When he didn't answer his phone, I called Onyx.

"Yo," Onyx answered.

"Hey, will you be able to tell Mother and Father that I won't be able to make it tonight? I have to take care of something."

"You already know that you're going to have to come down here and talk to them yourself. I won't pass on any messages."

I should've known that would be his answer.

"All right. Thanks for nothing."

"No problem, bro."

I hung up and left my apartment to head to the club. I was sure my parents had made it there. It was eight o'clock in the evening and there was no sign of a rainstorm that night. As I was leaving my building, I heard a voice from behind me.

"Rain," she said sweetly.

I turned around to face Essence.

"Hey, I thought you weren't coming for another hour."

"I figured that I would come over now. I couldn't wait for Colette."

"Are you really trying to go to Versailles tonight?"

"I would like to. I was trying to think of places you and I could go to get away for a little bit. Where you headed?"

"I'm on my way to request the night off. You want me to still take off so we can hang out, right?"

Her amber-colored eyes lit up. "Yes, I would love that."

I flagged down a taxi and we rode down Boulevard de Clichy.

She rested her pretty little head on my shoulder. "I'm so tired. You know, Rain, I've been thinking...I really want to work things out with you. You seem like a sweet person and someone who would take care of me for the rest of my life without question. I want that..."

"Is that what you really want or are you just saying that?"

"I wouldn't say it to say it. I mean it."

"I'm waiting for you. Whenever you're ready, I'm right here."

"I'm glad we're getting the chance to get to know one another because I think you're all I could ever want in a man. I would've never thought I would have a life like this. I'll be young forever. I'm stronger, faster, and the power of my mind is amazing."

"One thing you have to remember is that we are much stronger than humans. We can rip out their hearts, decapitate them, and suck them dry. We are a human's worst nightmare. My family doesn't do any harm to them unless we have to. We aren't perfect and we have made mistakes when we were newborns. We used to have blood slaves before they started volunteering to give blood for money."

"Have you ever killed anyone?"

"Of course I have. It's an urge that vampires naturally have. We fight the urge because we don't want anyone to think that we are one of the bad ones."

The taxi stopped in front of Vaisseau along the strip of the dark, unlit alley. As soon as we stepped out, the smell of the soggy sewer jumped out. The stench was a little more putrid that night, but I ignored it. Essence, on the other hand, covered up her nose. Having sensitive senses was normal for us. She was going to have to get used to it.

She moved her eyes up to the club's vivid flashing red sign above our heads. When her eyes met mine, I smiled at her. She smiled back. We didn't have to walk into the club too far. My parents were over in the lounge area, talking to one another.

"Sorry to interrupt you guys, but I need to take the night off."

My parents exchanged uncomfortable looks. For a split-second, I could tell that they weren't happy to see Essence in my company.

My father responded, "Legend and Soleil will cover the bar. We'll be fine. Do whatever it is you have to do."

I tried to read their expressions some more, but they quickly adjusted and blocked their thoughts from me. I shrugged it off. "I'll see you tomorrow night."

Taking my hand in hers while in the back of the cab, she said, "I feel like I love you when I don't even know much about you. Am I under some type of spell?"

"I don't cast spells. So, what you feel are your own feelings."

"I have something else I need to ask you."

I was worried that whatever she had to ask might not be what I wanted to answer right away. I swallowed the hard lump that formed in my throat and played with the golden emblem that was around my neck. "Okay."

"Do you have any children hidden anywhere?"

"No... Vampires can't have children."

"What happened to your last wife? Colette told me you were married once."

"She was human and she died from old age."

"Anything else I need to know?"

"I told you everything about me. There are no secrets."

Essence got teary-eyed. "I didn't want to become...this..."

"I'm sorry. Again, I am... Listen, how I feel for you, doesn't mean you have to feel that way for me right now. I want you to tell me you love me when you feel ready."

"What if that never happens? Then, I'll be stuck as a vampire for the rest of my life without you."

"You'll always have me, Essence. It doesn't matter what you

decide. I know you feel something for me, so I'm not worried about that. In due time you are going to tell me you love me, so I'm not rushing you."

There was no way I was going to rush her and I wasn't going to let her stray too far or else some other vamp was going to make his move on her.

"Let's get out right here and take a stroll in the park," she said.

I looked around while the cab came to a red light. There was no way we were going to get out and take a stroll in that park. It was one that a very dark brood had taken over. They were called the Ravens, a rebellious group of vampires who were scavengers, and they murdered humans and terrorized any vampire that wasn't one of them.

"I'll take you to another park."

"What's wrong with that park?"

"It's not safe for us there. Don't ever go to that park."

She nodded and placed her head on my shoulder.

I was going to tell her about the Ravens when the time was right. I didn't want to spoil our mood with bad news. Then she would know the difference between them and us.

"There are so many rules to remember."

"You'll learn them all. It seems overwhelming at first, but you'll be fine. I'm here to guide you, so if you need to know anything, ask me."

I caressed her hair. She stared up into my eyes. As we stared at one another, I bent down and placed a kiss on her lips. Her hand grabbed the back of my head to kiss me deeper.

CHAPTER 15

LEGEND

I glanced over at Chantal before I headed out to work for the night. She seemed a little distant and there was something troubling behind those engaging brown eyes. I wanted to ask her what was wrong, but I refrained. I had concerns of my own.

I noticed she had been making many phone calls to the United States. I casually asked her about it, but she caught an immediate attitude and denied it, so I left it alone.

"Legend?"

"Yes."

"What time will you be home tonight?" she asked.

"The same time I'm home every night. We close at two a.m.."

Her brain went elsewhere for a second as she played in her hair. "Legend, I've been thinking."

"About?"

"I have something to tell you, but I don't want you to get upset."

"Okay..." I was hoping she would finally talk about the phone calls.

"I contacted my family to tell them that I'm okay."

"You did what?" I scowled.

"You told me that no one could ever know and that I would have to be a missing person until they figure that I'm dead...but, I can't do that to my family."

"When did you talk to them?"

"I talked to my mommy. I told her that I'm still in Paris and that I'm okay."

I took a deep breath. If her parents decided to come looking for her, that wouldn't be a good thing.

"When is your best friend Jade coming by?"

"I told her that I wouldn't be going back with her because I fell for someone… But, I really want to avoid her altogether."

"Look, you can't talk to anyone else in your family. The vampires of Pigalle Palace live by a covenant and it is strict. We can be killed if the Préfet finds out that you are making human contact with your family members… Look, I need you to understand how serious this is."

"But I can't leave them hanging like this. I want to tell them the truth."

Anger rose in me. "You can't tell them the truth."

She turned away from me.

I sensed something in her. I felt as if she were hiding something from me.

"What else is going on?"

"Nothing."

"Don't lie to me. I can tell when you're lying to me."

"I promise you, nothing."

"There's something you're not telling me."

"I have nothing to hide."

I read her. She was definitely hiding something.

CHAPTER 16

ONYX

Soleil and I were on fire for one another. Sex, sex, sex, sex and more sex. She was ready any time and any place. I didn't mind it. If she wasn't at my place, then I was at hers. We even started having sex up in the rooms while at work.

One night, Soleil walked from my bathroom into my kitchen looking a little paler than her normal lifeless look. I raised a shot of vodka at her while standing at the kitchen island. She refused to drink with me by shaking her head no. Usually, she would be right with me shot for shot.

"What's the matter, sexy? You're not drinking with me tonight?"

She shook her head slowly. "Not tonight."

I took the shot. Then I kissed her, ready to get her in the bedroom. She backed all the way up, away from me as if my liquored-up kisses bothered her.

"What's up?"

"I really need to talk to you, Onyx."

"I'm all ears." I leaned my back up against the kitchen island.

She struggled with what she wanted to say next. She shook her golden, curly mane with both of her hands—something she did when she had a lot on her mind. She positioned herself between my legs so she could be closer. She put one hand on my scar and the other one on the other cheek. "This may sound crazy, but I'm pregnant."

"What did you say?"

She dropped her head, hands, as sudden tears poured from her beautiful eyes.

I lifted her head with my hands. "Soleil," I said gently. "Calm down."

"How is this possible, Onyx?"

"Are you really pregnant?"

"Yes, I can feel it inside of me."

She took my hand and placed it on her stomach. She was round.

"You're serious… What in the hell is going on?"

She shrugged her shoulders while rubbing the top of my legs with both of her hands. "What are we going to do?"

"I have to take you to Mother and Father. They will know what to do."

"No," she replied terrified. "They'll kill me. When was the last time you heard of a vampire getting pregnant?"

It was something that hadn't been done in centuries.

"I know."

"What's going to happen to us?"

I gently pulled both of her hands around my waist. "I guess we're going to have to find out."

"Do you really think that would be wise? Your parents will find out we're messing around. I'm going to lose my job. I have bills to pay."

I didn't know what we were going to tell Mother and Father, but we were going to have to tell the truth.

She placed her head on my chest. "This is all very scary."

"It is."

A wave of excitement filled me through the fear. Being a father was something that hadn't ever crossed my mind. The last full-blooded vampire ruled Pigalle Palace. His name was King Allemand and his body was in a hidden tomb beside that of his wife. They were both Daywalkers, vampires that could walk around in the sun.

Was our child the next to rule? Would our child be a Daywalker? That would mean that Rain may not be the one The Divination spoke of. It would mean our bloodline wasn't waiting for Rain, but for my seed.

"What are people going to say about me? About us?" she asked.

I wiped her tears as they continued to fall. "What we have is between us. Besides, our baby is going to be handsome. Don't you think? I mean, his daddy is handsome."

She laughed a little through her tears. "You're so full of yourself."

"I'm not… I think you should have little Onyx."

"Little Onyx? What if it's a girl?"

"It's a boy," I declared, going with my gut feeling.

She touched her stomach. I did, too. What we had created was something like a miracle.

"What am I going to do with you, Onyx?"

"Love me forever."

"I think I can fall in love with you in one day." She kissed me.

"Are you sure you're not in love already? You kiss me like you love me."

I rubbed her stomach again and imagined my son growing inside her.

"I am in love with you."

I hummed, "Mmm-hmm, I knew it. I love you, too."

"Why are you so sweet to me?"

"Mother raised this knucklehead the best she could."

"She raised an excellent knucklehead. Thank her for me."

"You can thank her yourself."

"So what are you going to tell the family?" A hint of agony replaced her happiness. "I hope it's as easy as you're making it seem."

"There is a certain way to approach my parents about certain things. Have you ever known love like this?"

"I've only been in love once and it was with my high school sweetheart. We were engaged. I told him that I was half-blooded because I didn't want to hide any secrets from him. One night, I was walking home from bartending and I was attacked and bitten by a vampire. He would've killed me if he hadn't been scared off by the police officer. I transformed in the hospital. The sun coming through the window burned my skin and that's how I knew. I found out later that my fiancé sent the vampire to kill me."

"One of your parents was a human?"

"Yes, my mother. Maybe that's why this happened?"

"Why do you think that?"

"Because we both were born to human women."

"Could be..I won't hurt you, Soleil. Those days are long gone. I'm going to show you a whole new definition of love."

She rubbed the scarred side of my face. "You want to tell me how that scar got there now?"

I was ready to tell her. I took a deep breath and replied, "I have one memory from when I was about eleven years old. I was playing outside of the house and some men came. They were looking for my birth mother and father. One of them grabbed me by the neck to make my parents come outside. He held the knife to my face and cut me. My mother came outside and begged them not to kill me. He flung me to the ground and I watched them kill her and then my father. My godparents appeared like out of nowhere, killed the men, and saved me and my siblings…"

Soleil continued to caress my face with tears in her eyes. "I hope our son looks just like you."

I ran my fingers through her curly mane. "He will."

She giggled. "You're supposed to say that he will look like me."

"Why would I lie to you?"

She laughed and I laughed with her to ease the sad mood.

"Our child will be beautiful no matter what because he is ours," I said. "Now, give me a kiss.

Soleil had been sick the past few mornings after she broke the news to me. She didn't feel well enough to try to hunt animals to feed on, so I told her we would get a thermal of donated blood from the club.

When we arrived at the club, Mother and Father were already there. When I saw them, nervousness swirled inside of me. I wanted to be the one to tell them what we had done, but I could tell by the look on Mother's face that she had already known.

As soon as my mother took one look at Soleil, her large eyes amplified as if she'd seen a ghost.

"Do you want me to go grab a thermal?" Soleil asked nervously.

Mother's eyes nearly came out of her head. She shot up quickly from her seat and swiftly levitated before us. Father was right behind her.

"Mother… Father," I said calmly.

Mother examined Soleil from her hair to her manicured fingernails. Soleil's skin was glowing as if she were alive. Entranced by her glow, my parents couldn't take their eyes off Soleil.

"She's *pregnant*," Mother said. "I see it."

"How is that possible?" Father asked.

"I don't know," I said. "But it's true and it's possible."

Soleil froze and didn't utter a word.

"Impossible." Mother casually laughed it off as if she were in denial.

"Soleil is my girlfriend and I want to protect her and the baby."

"Are you trying to tear what's left of this family apart?" Mother asked with tears coming to her eyes.

"No. We've never seen a vampire pregnant. This has to mean something."

"Never mind the meaning. How did this happen? Did you cast a spell or something?"

"We don't know any spells to cast, Mother. My siblings and I were born to a human. She was born to a human, too. Do you think that has something to do with it?"

Mother threw her back toward us. It still bothered her that we weren't her birth children. Whenever we spoke of our birth mother, she always got sensitive about it.

I added, "The Divination spoke of a Daywalker... Maybe we were wrong about Rain. Maybe he isn't the one. Maybe it will be my baby."

"How dare you curse the Divination," Father yelled. "You don't know better than any of us."

"When have you seen Rain walk in the sun? When have you seen Rain fulfill or carry out anything that was said in the Divination? Soleil is pregnant with a child that has the same DNA as our family. The Divination must've been talking about this child."

"This is outrageous," Mother nearly screamed. "The *Préfet* will not understand how this happened. We've managed to break almost every rule of Pigalle Palace as of recently. We won't have enough time to explain anything to them once they discover this. We can't expose this. We will be killed."

"Why should we hide?" I retorted. "Why would the Préfet be upset about something that they've been waiting for?"

"Get me out of here before I snatch his head off his body," Mother said.

Father followed behind her without saying another word. With tears in my eyes, I watched the both of them until they vanished around the corner.

"Do you think the Préfet will be upset? What do you think they'll do to us?"

Fear was in her eyes; I could see it.

I reached for her hands. "I'll protect you. I'll do whatever it takes to protect the both of you."

"Maybe we should abort the baby."

"No, I can feel that something very special is going to happen. So, calm down, baby," I said, rubbing both of her arms.

Soleil took a deep breath for a second before she asked, "I'm your girlfriend?"

"Aren't you?"

"When did I get that title?"

"You're having my baby, aren't you?"

"Just because I'm having your baby doesn't make me your girl-friend."

"You know what your problem is, Soleil?"

A wild fire was in her eyes. "What's my problem?"

"You think too much. I want this baby and I want you. Know that. Believe that."

She rolled her eyes, but I saw a small smile ease at the corners of her mouth. She wanted me to confirm what she already knew. Soleil was officially my woman.

CHAPTER 17

RAIN

"*What is this?*" Essence asked, flipping out over her iPad while sitting at the kitchen table. "My professors have reported me as a missing person."

She nearly spilled over the vase full of flowers with her rage. Even though she swore she wasn't concerned with anyone looking for her, she kept her nose in the news to see if she would turn up in it. Sometimes, she laughed at the news and sometimes, she cried. I didn't know why she worked herself up over that crap. Rumors were the only things those journalists believed in and they actually convinced the world it was the truth. They never apologized when they gave out false information, either.

I had just arrived home from work. I wasn't in the mood to fight with her, especially when we were finally trying to bond as a married couple.

"I need to show back up at school," she said.

"You can take night classes like Colette. She's learned to go to different campuses, so no one would think anything funny."

"I guess that's the only choice I have. That means I would have to withdraw out of my day classes. This is so messed up. I'm going to have to move back into my dorm."

"You don't have to live back on campus."

"That's the only way my life will feel normal again. Will you be able to come by and visit?"

I sighed at the thought of being restricted from her company. This wasn't going my way. I started walking toward the front door.

"Where are you going?"

"I have to get some air."

"What are you doing here?" Onyx asked, opening his front door for me.

I spent my whole day thinking until I couldn't focus anymore. It was almost nine o'clock at night on a Sunday and we were going to have to be at the club in an hour. I took off my shoes at the door and followed him inside.

"Essence read her missing person's report today."

He frowned. "Didn't you explain to her that she would be filed as a missing person if she didn't go back to school?"

"I told her, but she wants to go back to school, and she wants me to give her the space to do what makes her comfortable."

"How are you really feeling? It doesn't seem like you and the new bride are getting along too well."

"This is all becoming more complicated than it needs to be."

"I'm sure this was what Father meant when he said we had to choose our brides carefully…"

"That's exactly what I was thinking on my way over here."

"Well, I have some news to share," Onyx announced.

"Yeah? What's that?"

"I got Soleil pregnant."

"Soleil? The bartender?"

"Yeah…"

I frowned deeply. "Wait, is that even possible?"

"Mother gave her an ultrasound earlier this evening… Yes, there's a baby and he or she is growing."

This couldn't be true. He had to be joking. "Yeah right."

"I swear to you."

As I tried to process the news, Soleil walked into the kitchen and Onyx's face lit up.

I thought we were in the house alone. She actually startled me a little bit. I straightened up and waved. *"Bonsoir, Soleil."*

"Bonsoir, Rain. How are you?"

"I'm good. How are you?"

"I'm doing pretty well."

"Congratulations on the baby."

"Thank you." She held on to Onyx.

Onyx kissed the side of her face.

"I'm going to head to the club. Thanks for being an ear, Onyx," I said. "I'll see you there."

"No problem, bro. I'm here for you whenever you need me."

This would be the very first vampire-born baby in over two centuries. Worry filled me. It was time for me to face the one thing I had been running away from, the Divination.

CHAPTER 18

LEGEND

went into the living room and the sliding door to the balcony was opened. Chantal went out to view the city as the lights twinkled underneath the moonlight.

I joined her. "Hey, baby? What you out here thinking about?"

"I'm just thinking…"

"I can see that. What's on your mind?"

She hesitated for a moment as if she didn't want to tell me. After a few seconds of silence, she said, "I don't think I'm ready for this."

"You don't think you're ready for what?"

"Is there a way to turn me back human?" She took off her wedding ring and placed it in my hand.

I stared down at the ring, feeling very confused. I scowled deeply. "This is not a game, Chantal. This is irreversible. I thought this was something you wanted."

"I can't do this anymore. I'm going back to Chicago."

Seemed like her mind was made up. There was no point in arguing with her.

"When?"

"Tomorrow night."

"You do know that the life you used to know is no more, right? No one there will understand the change in you. Vampires aren't accepted like that over there, and you will find that you will start to hate them. You might even kill a few of them. See, Pigalle Palace isn't just a place of erotic indiscretion. It's our home. The only place we can be safe in."

Chantal shrugged. "I don't care. I want to go home. I don't belong here."

"So, you don't plan on coming back?"

Her eyes became vacant, empty, and she seemed to space out. "...No."

I chewed on the inside of my jaw to contain the sadness my heart instantly felt. "I see you gave this some thought?"

"Of course I did. I jumped into this head first without much thought about my life back at home. I can't stop thinking about home."

I went inside, poured some Brandy in a glass from the bar, and placed her ring on the countertop.

"Thank you for everything you've done for me," she said as she came inside.

My mind felt caught in a whirlwind as I tried to find a trace of sadness or any tears in her eyes. Nothing told me she really wanted to be with me. I swallowed the hard lump in my throat and prepared myself for the breakup.

"Go ahead and leave. Make sure that you leave everything that belongs to me here."

She fluttered her eyelashes and frowned as if to ask how I could be so cold all of a sudden. She took out the card from her purse and placed it on the bar next to the ring, looking at me in a way I didn't recognize. What'd she think? I wasn't going to let her still have access to my money while she was away.

"I was hoping I could still use this for a few more weeks, to help me get another place and what not once I get home."

I cocked my head to the right slightly and stared at her. She was crazy. "Why would I let you do that?" I picked up the card and waved it in front of her face. "You do have money to get you home without me, right?"

"Don't, Legend..."

"Why not leave right now? Why wait until tomorrow?"

"You want me to leave right now?"

"Why not? Since you're so unhappy."

"So, you're going to be a jackass about this and put me out?"

"I think you should leave right now before I lose my cool with you."

"I still have another twenty-four hours..."

"I'm not giving you twenty-four hours. I want you to leave right now. Do you need some money to go to a hostel?" I drank and poured more.

"A hostel? Are you serious? You can't be serious."

"Oh, I'm dead serious."

"Don't play games right now."

"You don't play games. You pull this insane antic on me after I made a very serious commitment to you and you expect me to be nice about it. Trust me when I say that this was a big mistake."

"So, this is now the Legend show. Well, let me be the one to break it to you, baby. This is about me, too. ...I'll go ahead and leave right now." She turned to walk away.

"Hey, I don't beg women to stay. I can get any woman I want."

She spun around quickly. "Then go get her."

After I grabbed the ring and the debit card, I stormed off to my bedroom. I placed them on the dresser in my bedroom. I took off all my clothes except for my boxers before getting in the bed. I needed some sleep.

Chantal walked in and went into the bathroom. I heard her flush the toilet before she washed her hands and turned off the light. She stopped at the dresser briefly before she lay in the bed next to me, not touching me at first, but then took her hands and placed them in my boxers to rub my dick. She let out a subtle moan as she rested her face, soaked with tears, in the crook of my neck against my dreads.

"Legend," she managed to say through her sniffles. "Don't let me go."

That was all she had to say to soften my heart.

She was becoming my world and it almost felt like my new world was going to end if she left it. Therefore, she stayed.

CHAPTER 19

ONYX

"Hey, you," Soleil greeted me from behind the bar as she cleaned glasses to prep for the night.

Even though she had just left my bed, seeing her face at work was like seeing her for the first time in a long time.

"How are you feeling? Is the baby giving you any problems?"

"No, the baby is doing just fine. Kicking me like crazy, though."

"You look beautiful as always."

"Thank you, my love."

I wanted to pull her over the bar and land a huge kiss, but that would've been inappropriate. I let my thoughts do all the imagining.

"Have you talked to Azura yet?" she asked.

"Yeah. I talked to her. She supports whatever we want to do."

"That's good."

I leaned over the bar and placed a kiss on her lips briefly. I couldn't help myself. Her glossed lips were begging me to touch them.

Rain cleared his throat from behind me. "We have a family meeting upstairs. Right now."

I nodded and winked at her. "I'll see you later."

"I'll be right here," she replied.

I headed to the elevator with Rain.

"You're one lucky man," he stated. "I never noticed how hot Soleil was before you starting messing with her."

"Keep not noticing, my brotha, because she's all mine."

"Are you nervous about the pregnancy?"

"Of course I am. I'm worried about what the Préfet will say."

"I understand you on that. Well, the pressure is definitely more on me now. That's for sure. Do you realize how hard it's been for me? It's too much pressure."

"Rain, can I ask you something?"

"What's up?"

"Have you tried daywalking?"

Rain answered honestly, "Not yet."

"Then, how do you know that you can't?"

He became silent. Rain and his damned silence was irritating. Rain was afraid to take responsibility and face it. He wanted to be free and do whatever he pleased, but time was ticking and he needed to be King if that was his true destiny.

The Divination said that one from our bloodline would reign over Pigalle Palace. He would be the one to finally rule after the murder of King Allemand and his wife, Queen Christione. All broods would have to obey the laws of the new King. Rain wasn't ready for that.

We entered the conference room. Father was sitting at the head of the round table with Mother, Legend, and Azura. We joined them.

"I called this family meeting because our family is on the brink of self-destruction," Father said. "If we don't act fast, we all won't be shown any mercy and beheaded. So, I want to address these matters. Let's start with Rain. I hear Essence is returning to school."

Rain immediately spoke, "She has and I've told her everything to keep a low profile."

"Do you really think that's going to work?" Mother questioned.

"I'm keeping a very close eye on her," Rain shot back defensively.

"There's something you should know, my son," Mother said. "If I'm correct, Essence has broken the marriage by sleeping with another man."

Rain tilted his head to the side. "No, she hasn't. I keep a very close eye on my wife."

"Your wife is no longer your wife, Rain."

Rain's chest heaved up and down. "Bullshit."

"I have facts and as your mother, you will respect me. You lower your voice when you speak to me."

"I will never disrespect you, Mother. Let me talk to her. I'm sure this is all one big misunderstanding."

"There's no misunderstanding. Trust what I tell you."

Rain sat back in his chair. I never saw Rain look so defeated. He was always so poised and so confident.

"Legend," Father said.

"Yes, Father."

"You're the first born and out of everyone, we expect you to know better than to accidentally change a strange woman into one of us… I question your state of mind when you committed this accident. Chantal is trying to go back to a normal human life from what I hear as well," Father said.

"She was going through a phase, but that's over now," Legend said.

"Why do you think Chantal is so eager to get back to Chicago?" Father asked with a frown.

"I don't know."

"Did you know that Chantal has a husband already?" Mother asked.

"She's not married."

"You didn't check."

"She wasn't wearing a wedding ring the night we met."

"Did you ask her?"

"Of course not," Legend replied.

"Maybe you should've because she's very much married and he's trying to locate her as we speak. He's the reason why she wants to go back to her old life."

"She can't go back to him," Legend said.

"You need to let her go," Father asserted.

Mother looked worried. "The Préfet isn't going to like this at all..."

"Why would the government be so upset about any of this?" Rain asked, leaning back into the chair.

"Turning the wrong humans into vampires can start a war between the humans and vampires. We stay in our own community for a reason. You want a wife, then you get a vampire. We have so many great resources. You two forced these women to do what they didn't want to do, and now we all have to suffer the consequences of your actions," Father bellowed.

"I didn't force Essence," Rain replied.

"You can be in denial all you want, Rain. The truth is the truth. She didn't willingly let you suck her blood. You seduced her. You mesmerized her and then took what you wanted," Mother said.

Rain didn't respond.

"Chantal begged for me to turn her," Legend stated.

Mother shifted in her seat. "Regardless, she didn't mean it. I want you all to listen to me. We have to end this now and you all know what we must do."

Silence ate up the room for a few moments. They were moving down the line, in no particular order of birth. They were addressing what needed to be addressed. I was going to be next. I had created the biggest mishap—a child.

"Onyx," Father said.

"Yes, Father."

"You're challenging the Divination. You have managed to do something that hasn't been done for centuries. You and Soleil are expecting a child that has half the DNA that you two share… For that reason, you believe your child will be a Daywalker."

"I don't challenge the Divination," I replied, "But, isn't that what happened the last time a vampire child was conceived? He was our last King. He was a Daywalker."

"Yes, your child will automatically be viewed as royalty around here. If, in fact, your child is born a Daywalker, he or she will be the new King or Queen of Pigalle Palace without question. The Préfet will want to test this out, of course. As soon as the baby is born, we will have to take the child to them and they will expose the child to the sun. If the child burns, they will continue to let the child burn to death."

"What?" I asked.

"That's the way it has to be, son."

Before I could finish my protest, Mother spoke over me, "Another thing. We have to kill Chantal and Essence."

"No!" Rain stood up. "I won't kill my wife!"

Father exploded, "Sit your ass down!"

Rain sat reluctantly.

"Essence is no longer your wife! She has broken the bond! She must die!" Father shouted.

"Let me talk to her, please. Essence wouldn't do anything like that to me."

"Fine… Do what you think is best," Mother answered. "We'll keep everything under control on our end and we'll try to mask all of this by staying quiet. That means that none of your women can be in this club. Soleil can no longer work the bar. She will start showing soon. These women must stay hidden. If any of these women go against what we are ordering, I'll rip their heart outs myself."

"Anything you would like to address me about?" Azura asked.

"The only thing I want you to do," Father answered, "is look after your brothers. If you see anything suspicious or feel anything suspicious, you tell us."

"Of course."

"Are we done here?" Rain asked in an irritated tone.

"That's it," Father replied.

We all stood. Legend, Rain, and I filed out of the room, leaving our parents and Azura to themselves. Rain was quiet as we walked down the corridor. Essence was a very sensitive subject for him and anything regarding the Divination as well. He had been too wound up and was becoming too unpredictable.

The government was growing tired of ruling Pigalle Palace. We were in need of a King.

I broke the silence. "What was that about, Rain? You accused our parents of being wrong. When have they ever been wrong?"

"They are controlled by the Préfet."

"The Préfet has done nothing but protect us since the King was murdered."

"Who gives a flying fuck about the Préfet? I'm so sick of living by their fucked-up rules," Rain exploded. "This is our family. The government is stupid. If the women we choose decide to leave us, who cares?"

"Everything has an order, brother," Legend spoke up. "You do understand that the Préfet can kill us, right?"

"Do you really think they'll do that? When was the last time you heard about them executing a vampire?" Rain questioned.

"It's been hundreds of years; yet, they do have the power to do whatever they want to do. We would stand trial. I have to be honest; this whole ordeal that we've created can start a war," I said.

Rain was silent and Legend ran his hand through his dreads as we proceeded to the elevator.

I said, "I'm going to have to break the news to Soleil. This is going to be tough for us. She may want to have an abortion now."

"Don't let her do that. She can't have an abortion," Rain replied. "She could possibly be carrying our next King."

I didn't think I would hear Rain admit that. If she were carrying our next King, then Rain wouldn't be the chosen one after all.

We walked out of the elevator to the front of the club.

"Soleil and I are going out for a little bit. You want to go?"

"Nah, I'm going to stock the bar," Rain responded.

"What about you, Legend?"

"I have to go see about Chantal."

"Understood," I replied.

Soleil's eyes were bright and she wore an incredible smile on her face as soon as our eyes met. An elegant goddess was standing before me and I felt like I was in heaven.

"You ready to go, baby?" I asked her.

"Let's go."

Soleil lay in my lap as we watched some sappy love movie she had been dying to see. I was more of an action kind of person, so the movie wasn't holding my attention whatsoever.

I bent down so I could give her an upside-down kiss while my hands traveled from her stomach to her breasts.

"Baby, watch the movie," she said, pushing my hands away.

"I'd rather watch your sexy ass in the bedroom than this horrible movie right now."

I maneuvered around so I could be on top of her. She giggled as I covered her face with more wet kisses.

"Cut it out, Onyx. Let's watch this movie for once."

The phone rang. I let her go saying, "Saved by the phone."

"You want me to get it?"

"Sure."

She answered, "Hello..." She frowned while she listened to whoever it was on the other end.

"Who is it?" I asked, reading her dazed expression.

"Your mother."

I took the phone from her. "Mother?"

"Onyx?"

"Yes."

"Have you seen Rain?"

The panic in her voice startled me. "I haven't seen him since I left the club. What's wrong?"

"I can't find him. Legend thinks he may have gone to the university to look for Essence."

"What? I thought you told him to stay away from the campus right now."

"Rain hasn't been himself lately. This is the second time he's been to her dorm since I gave him direct orders."

"I'll go find him."

"Good. Let me know what happens when you return."

I hung up the phone and rushed to the door.

"Onyx," Soleil called after me.

"I'll be right back."

"Where are you going?" A worried look covered her face.

I kissed her forehead. "I have to go find Rain."

I waited in the shadows on the rooftop of the dorm where Essence and Colette stayed. It was close to 9 p.m. and I spotted Rain following Essence. Why was he stalking this woman?

As soon as Essence disappeared inside of the building, I jumped down from the roof and crept up behind Rain. He felt my presence and turned around.

"How'd you know I was here?" he asked.

"Mother called me. What are you doing here, Rain?"

"I'm here to make sure Essence is safe and I need to make sure that she's not seeing anyone else..."

"You've got to be kidding me. What are you going to do if she is seeing another man? Then what?"

"I will rip him to pieces."

"That's not in your character, Rain. You might as well let her go."

Rain stepped close to me and got in my face. "I won't ever let her go. I love her too much."

"There's nothing you can do about this. Rain, you might as well let Mother kill her."

"I won't let Mother kill her, Onyx. Are you not my brother? I need you to have my back on this. What if this were Soleil, we were standing here talking about? I don't see you killing your child and I don't see you killing her."

I understood once Rain put it that way. I would pay for it later to go against our parents, but I had to trust him and have his back. "Let me know if you need my help."

CHAPTER 20

RAIN

I knocked on Essence's dorm room right after Onyx went back home. He needed to trust me to handle my situation. I didn't need any one of them holding my hand through my own mess. I'd created it, so I was going to fix it. If Essence didn't want to be with me, then I was going to have to deal with letting her go.

Essence opened the door for me with a look of surprise. "Rain… What are you doing here?"

"I can't go another day without seeing you. Can I come in?"

She opened the door wider, so I could walk in. "You see me, so what do you want?"

Her beautiful face wore a frown as her thick, poignant voice was like music to my ears.

A soulful slow beat from her iPod greeted me as soon as the door was closed.

"How long are you going to stay away from me?" I asked.

"Not too much longer."

"I need an exact time frame. We are married and we have to make our bond stronger. You have to stay by your husband's side. Do you understand that?" I sat on a chair that was in the corner of the room.

"I love the way that sounds, Rain… However, you didn't give me much of a choice that night when you bit me. I never asked or agreed to become…this…"

I leaned back in the chair and rubbed my chin. "I understand, but I really wish you'd get over it. I don't want you to keep holding that over my head forever. I want you to love me the way that I love you. Right now, you're not connecting with me the way you should. That makes me believe that you've broken our bond. Have you slept with anyone else, Essence?"

She didn't blink or stutter. In fact, it was as if she had been dying to tell me the truth all along. "Yes..."

I took a deep breath and exhaled. "Why?"

She shrugged. "I just did."

"Who is he?"

"I can't tell you that."

"Is he human?"

"No."

With a deep frown, I badgered, "Another vampire?"

"Yes."

"Does he know that you're married?"

"Yes, he knows everything."

I didn't need to hear any more. There was no need to find out who this other vampire was. Instead of cutting her head off or ripping her heart out, which I could've done at that very moment, I fled from her dorm.

CHAPTER 21

AZURA

As soon as I got home from closing the club, Onyx called. I rarely came home alone. My male companion had his hands all over my ass. All I was trying to do was get him into my room so I could fuck him. With my annoying phone ringing from my pocket nonstop, I had to answer it. Only someone in my family would be trying to get to me so desperately.

"Hold on, baby," I said. "My cell is ringing."

I reached in my pocket to retrieve my phone. It was Onyx. *"Bonsoir, mon frère."*

"Have you heard from Legend or any news about Chantal?"

"No. Why? What's up?"

"He's not answering his phone. I just met Chantal's husband in the alley while leaving Vaisseau."

"Uh-oh. What did you tell him?"

"I told him I never heard of Chantal. He proceeded to tell me that he was going to find her with or without my help."

I walked over to my couch and sat down, signaling my lover for the night to hold on. "Holy shit. Do you think he knows anything about us? He came right to the club. How did he know where to start searching for her?"

"She came to Paris with her best friend, Jade. From what Legend told me, Jade had to return to Chicago without Chantal. I'm sure

Jade told Chantal's husband everything she knew. She came to the club with Chantal, and she saw Chantal go home with Legend."

"I was afraid this would happen."

"We have to warn Legend."

"Did you try to go over to his place?" I asked.

"Not yet, but I need to."

"We can't let Mother and Father know anything about this."

"Exactly. Get some rest," Onyx said.

"All right. I'll talk to you later."

He hung up and I asked my male lover for the night, "You ready?" He nodded.

"Bring your sexy ass over here."

CHAPTER 22

RAIN

At times, I wondered if my family set the standards too high since I couldn't completely live up to the standard that was set for me. I planned to test the theory about my day-walking powers one day, but not until I felt like it. Other things were on my mind—like Essence breaking our bond.

I spent days upset, pacing, and confusion had my mind warped. I didn't answer my phone. I didn't go to work. I didn't want to be bothered.

I walked slowly to the bathroom to run hot water for a shower. The doorbell rang. I walked down the hallway to see who was at the door. When I looked through the peephole, I couldn't believe she was standing there with sunglasses on. I whisked the door opened to face her.

"What the fuck do you want?" I roared.

"Can we talk for a minute?" Essence asked.

"We have nothing to talk about. You slept with another man. That means you are free to do what you please. Leave me the fuck alone."

"At least let me tell you how it happened."

"I don't care about how it happened."

"Please…"

I leaned against the side of wall. "Why aren't you with him?"

She removed her shades revealing her red puffy eyes. "I don't want to be with him. I never wanted to be with him. I made a mistake... Look, Rain, I'm so sorry."

I opened the door wider and let her in, though I shouldn't have. "I'm listening."

She looked behind me as she could hear the water running from the bathroom. "Am I disturbing your shower?" she asked.

"I'm going to get in the shower as soon as you leave."

"...Let me take a shower with you."

She took the liberty to walk down the hallway as if I said it were okay. I followed her to the steamy bathroom anyway.

Without saying another word to one another, I undressed her slowly. Silent tears fell from her eyes. She undressed me next. We got in the hot shower kissing, washing, and massaging one another. It was as if the hot water was washing away her sin. I had a forging heart. That was my nature. I didn't care about any mistakes she made because I loved her unconditionally.

She didn't have to ask me to make love to her. Her body had been begging to be touched by me the moment she walked into my door. As soon as I entered into her pillow-like moist center, I felt as if I never wanted to get out of her. We were resolidifying.

"You belong to me," I said, thrusting into her most tender place.

"Yes... I don't want anyone else, but you."

"Are you sure about that?"

"Yes.... Oh, yes... Baby, I'm yours. This pussy is yours."

My ego needed to hear that. As we climaxed, we shared an orgasm. We got out of the shower and lay in the bed. For a few minutes, we were silent. For some reason, I sighed loudly, when my thoughts became too heavy. Would I really be the last man? I wasn't sure if I could trust her ever again.

"Look, he meant nothing," she said, reading my mind.

"I don't want to talk about him."

She stared at me oddly with her head cocked to the side. "How can you say you forgive me if you think I will cheat on you again?"

"I forgive you, but I won't forget."

"So, what happens between us now?"

"We have to go to my parents and they'll tell us what to do next."

"Why do your parents have to be our guide? How come we can't do whatever we want to do?"

"Because we can't. From now on, we have to follow all of the rules."

"I want us to start all over, Rain. I really do, but I want you to make our own decisions. I want us to make our own decisions. I'll see you later."

"Where are you going?"

"Back to the dorm."

"What? Oh, hell no. I won't let you use me for sex, Essence. I don't play these types of games. Either you're here with me or you're not."

She kissed the side of my face. "I'll come back to see you to-morrow."

"You better stay right here."

She chuckled. "Are you afraid I won't return?" She straddled me. "I love your kisses. I love the way your hands make me quiver. I can wake up to them every day. Just not right now. I need more time."

She traced my lips with her tongue. Essence started to grind a little, rubbing back and forth against me. I moved my hands to her big breasts and then put my mouth on one of her nipples. She moaned as I took the other one as well. Then, I was back to kissing her.

I felt myself growing hard again. She aligned her center and I inched my way inside. Something about Essence drove me wild. I squeezed her soft flesh and touched wherever my hands could touch.

She moaned loudly and screamed to the heavens. Her sex expression was sultry and sexy. There was no stopping her as she bounced harder and faster. She exploded like a fountain when we were done.

"You're such an incredible lover," she said.

"Is that what you like most about me?"

"Yes. I'm guilty." She had an evil laugh.

That's when I first noticed it. Essence was crossing over to the dark side. I stared at her with disbelief. At that moment, I wasn't so sure I could make Essence conform to doing anything my way. Once a newborn had evil inside of them, they became stronger and the worst type of vampire—fatal.

My family was held in high regard in Pigalle Palace. If Essence tapped into her evil instincts, and if I were truly the one, then my venom would make her as powerful as me.

Ultimately, I was going to have to kill her before she got too strong.

"You want me to take you back to your dorm?"

"You trying to get rid of me?" she asked as she lightly played with my hands.

"Believe me. You'd know if I was trying to get rid of you."

She scooted as close to my body as she could.

"Essence," I heard myself say. "What is it that you've been truly feeling lately? Any bad thoughts?"

"All types of things have been running in my mind."

She giggled with a devilish grin.

I didn't show her how alarmed I was feeling. I was definitely going to have to keep a very close eye on her.

CHAPTER 23

LEGEND

I got up from my slumber about 5:06 p.m.. I eased out of bed to find Chantal cooking in the kitchen. Cooking wasn't really my thing; I didn't like to eat food. Some vampires could still eat, but I preferred to drink all my meals.

"You feel like eating today, I see." I kissed her on the cheek.

She replied, "I really miss cooking. I may eat a little of it, so it won't go to waste… I really miss cooking…"

She was acting as if we had money to toss down the drain. Even though we had more than enough money, everything my family worked for, we preserved.

I sat on a barstool at the counter as I watched her work around the kitchen. I could tell that when she was human, she was a great cook.

"Jade hasn't answered her phone all morning," she said.

"Maybe she's been busy."

"I think she's upset with me. I think she's upset that I stayed here…with you."

"Did you ever have that talk with her?"

"I did and I told her that I was starting a new life… Anyway, I need some retail therapy. I'm going shopping."

"Chantal… We need to talk about your spending habits."

She ignored me and kept making the dinner as if I wasn't talking.

CHAPTER 24

ONYX

"What do you mean I can't work at the bar anymore?" Soleil asked.

"My parents decided that they would like to keep this pregnancy under wraps. It's nothing personal. They want to keep the Préfet out of this for as long as they can. If anyone at the bar spots your growing midsection, we'll be called to court."

"You're okay with their decision?"

"It's for the best. Plus, I don't have a choice."

"Where the hell am I supposed to hide out for nine months?"

"From what my mother researched, vampire births only last for half the time, so around five months, the baby will be ready for delivery."

"Where are we going to deliver?"

"My parents' mansion."

"So, this is what was discussed at the family meeting?"

"That…amongst other things."

She wrapped her arms around me and cradled her head into the crook of my neck.

"I'm terrified."

"Soleil, baby, you don't have to be afraid. We will be just fine."

"You're such a great man. Whatever is happening in my womb feels so magical."

"Really?"

"Yes, I feel like this baby has special powers."

"He might."

"He?"

"Yes, you heard me. I said 'he.' It's a boy. I felt this way the first time you told me you were pregnant. I dreamed of a son last night. That confirmed what I was feeling."

She smiled. "I think so, too."

We both smiled with joy.

Suddenly, Rain walked into my house without knocking.

"Rain?"

"Onyx, what the hell is going on around here?"

"What do you mean?"

Soleil could tell by the growling tone in Rain's voice that she didn't want to be a part of the conversation. She left the room to leave us to talk.

"Azura just called and told me that Chantal's husband is looking for her."

"Yeah, Chantal's husband came to the club looking for her and he asked me a bunch of questions. I told him I didn't know her."

"Does Legend know about this?"

"I haven't gotten a chance to talk to him and I'm not sure if Azura told him."

"We have to talk to him or at least warn him. Do you think Chantal knows?"

"Her husband didn't say anything about speaking with her, so… I doubt it."

Rain rubbed the top of his head. "Shit, this is getting crazy. I'm in trouble my damned self."

"Why you say that?"

"Essence is changing… She's not the sweet woman I met at Vaisseau."

"Of course she's changing. She's a vampire now."

"No, I mean she's a little dark...a little evil..."

I sat straight up. If he was suggesting that his precious little Essence was crossing over to the other side, then she was going to cause havoc. Having Rain's venom in her could give her super strength.

"What makes you think this?"

"The way she looks at me. I can see it in her eyes. I'm going to have to kill her."

"You should've killed her a few days ago when she was weaker. As the days go by, her strength will build. How is she surviving? Does she talk about her hunts?"

"I have no idea how she's getting her blood."

"We have to take care of all of this. Even if she crosses over, Rain, you have the power to destroy her. Why won't you tap into any of your powers? What are you afraid of, lil' brother? We are royalty. The Divination says that."

"Fuck the Divination!"

Lightning struck and a loud roaring thunder shook the house. I looked up at the ceiling as it cracked a little. I looked back at him.

"You see the kind of power you have when you're upset? We have to end this now and you're the only one that can do it."

Rain shook his head. "I'm not the only one. I'm just the beginning. Your son will be the one to end it. Trust me when I say that."

"We don't know that."

"I *know* that. Meeting tonight, thirty past midnight."

"Where?"

"Mother and Father's."

"All right," I replied.

"Bring Soleil."

"Will do."

He vanished.

I shook off the bad vibes Rain sprouted, but for some reason, I really couldn't get rid of the bad feeling. Thoughts of a war entered my mind.

Suddenly, Legend entered.

"We were just talking about you, Legend."

"Who are we?"

"Rain and me. He just left."

Legend looked as if he had been worried. "Oh really? What were you talking about?"

"We were talking about Chantal amongst other things. Nothing that you don't know about. Legend, you look like shit."

Legend's facial hair had grown into a rugged-looking shrub and his dreads were frizzy at the roots. His clothes looked as if he had tossed them on. The way he usually took his time when choosing clothing clearly went out the window that evening.

"I feel like shit. How are Soleil and the seed?"

"They're doing fine. How are things with you and Chantal?"

"I want her to disappear. She's spending up my money and she's doing things like cooking and then dumping the food. She complains about all the things she used to do that she can't do anymore like walk in the sun. Mother and Father want me to take her life, but if I couldn't do it the first time, what makes them think that I can do it this time?"

"Did you know that Chantal's husband is in Paris looking for her?"

"No," he replied with a frown. "This is the first I heard of it."

"Has she admitted to being married?"

"No and I haven't asked her. I'm afraid my anger will snap her little neck."

"Well, you've been warned and she does have another husband."

"If he finds her, then he finds her. Anyway, I'll handle it."

"Do what you got to do."

"We're all supposed to meet up at the mansion for a family meeting tonight. Are you coming?" Legend asked.

"Soleil and I will be there. Are you bringing Chantal?"

"Depends on how she's feeling about it. Is Rain bringing Essence?"

"I think so, but I'm not certain."

"I'll see you later."

Legend left and I went into the bedroom to check on Soleil. She was lying in the bed with her eyes closed.

"Are you sleeping?"

"No, resting. I'm concentrating on the butterflies fluttering in my stomach."

I smiled and lay next to her.

"You make me happy," she said.

"I'm glad because you make me happy, too."

"I really appreciate all you've done for me."

"It's no problem. My job now is to protect the both of you."

"Good."

"The club won't be open tonight. We're having a family meeting. They want you to come as well."

"Okay. Your family likes to have a lot of meetings."

"Yeah. With the new things going on, it's good to get together."

"Now that your mother is aware that I was born to a mortal, she acts like she doesn't like me."

"She likes you."

"She looks at me as if I'm a roach, scavenging after her son. She gives me the coldest looks, Onyx, and you know it."

"She looks at everyone that way."

Soleil rested up against me as I caressed the top of her head. I gently played with her wild golden hair. She kissed me with so much passion. I moaned and slipped my hands up her skirt. She unbuckled my pants. Her right hand immediately took me out and started working me.

I closed my eyes, relaxed, took my mind off our troubles, and concentrated on how Soleil was making me feel. I moaned closing my eyes tight as ecstasy took over my whole body. From the tip of my toes to the top of my head, I felt the pleasure she wanted me to endure.

When she opened her mouth to place me inside, it felt like heaven. I was already sensitive and ready to explode before Soleil even touched me. I let go thick and hot into her mouth in a matter of seconds. She swallowed me.

CHAPTER 25

RAIN

Essence made up an excuse not to come to my parents' house for the gathering. I showed up alone. My mother had invited one more guest I wasn't expecting to see: Olivia, my ex-girl-friend. She'd had a family emergency in New Orleans and had to leave Paris abruptly, but that was years ago. She never contacted me once she left and I had no way of contacting her. How did they get her to come back to Paris and why was she here after all these years?

Olivia was a few feet away, drinking and laughing with my mother. Her eyes sparkled as soon as she saw me. One of her best qualities was her blue eyes. For some reason when she turned into a vampire, her eyes turned blue instead of the amber or light-brown color that most vampires had.

I turned to Onyx. "What is she doing here?"

"They said she happened to stop by."

She happened to stop by? That was a lie. I felt this was my mother's doing. She hated Essence that much that she would go out of her way to bring Olivia back to get me to leave Essence alone.

Mother waved for me to come over and I walked to them.

"Hey," Olivia said, giving me a hug. "It's so good to see you, Rain."

"It's good to see you, too. This is a pleasant surprise," I lied.

Mother was grinning from ear to ear. She always liked Olivia for me and always hoped that we would get married one day. At one point, I was close to proposing, but she left abruptly. I hated her for doing that to me.

"She's so pretty," Father said, joining the conversation. "I always thought so. Don't you think so, Rain?"

"She's always been beautiful." That was the truth, but she meant nothing to me anymore.

"Thank you," Olivia replied with a bright smile.

"Why don't you two sit and catch up?" Mother asked while linking arms with Father.

Olivia and I sat on the couch next to Onyx and Soleil.

A server came around with champagne on a tray. I handed her a glass. We drank in silence. Olivia kept staring at me and I kept staring at her. Suddenly, all hate went out of the window. I wanted to tear all her clothes off immediately. My animalistic desires felt rampant and I was ready for them to take over. It was amazing that she could still do that to me after being gone for 300 years.

Olivia whispered in my ear, "I missed you."

"Is that so? What do you miss about me?"

"We used to have so much fun together. I want to kiss you right now."

I chuckled and shook my head while taking her hand in mine. "You've always been a quick mover."

"I want you in my mouth right now."

"You can do whatever you want to me…later."

I glanced across the room, and there was Essence. I removed my hand from Olivia's immediately. Essence smiled as we made eye contact.

Onyx cleared his throat and said, "Essence is here."

I then turned my attention to Olivia, whose undemanding angelic blue eyes were wide, curious, and almost afraid because Essence was within a few feet of us.

"Is that her?" Olivia questioned.

"Yeah. Excuse me."

I got up from the couch and before I could meet Essence, she was already standing in front of me with the confidence of a queen. She may have been the queen of her world, but it would be a cold day in hell when she would rule over me. I could feel her newfound power and though it was scary as hell, I stood there firmly.

"Rain." She fluttered her eyelashes as if she were expecting me to respond. She stood tall in her three-inch gold stilettos.

"What are you doing here?" I asked.

"I thought about it and changed my mind. I figured, why not come and mingle with my in-laws."

"If you were going to come, you should've come with me earlier. My parents don't like for guests to show up unannounced."

I looked across the foyer and my parents were staring at us.

"I hope they're not mad. They extended the invite in the first place, so I'm only a little late. They should feel pleased that I showed up at all." She flung her long hair over her shoulder in an awkward silence. The tension between the two of us was too profuse. Essence glared at Olivia and then smirked. "Who is she?"

"I need to talk to you, Rain," Mother demanded.

Mother looked at Essence as if she were an old chewed-up piece of gum on the bottom of her shoe.

"Hello, Mother. It's good to see you again," Essence said in a sneering tone.

"I need to talk to you now, Rain!" Mother exclaimed, walking to the library.

I turned to Olivia. "I'll be right back."

She smiled at me. "Okay."

Essence snapped her head from Olivia to me.

Olivia introduced herself to Essence. "Hello, I'm Olivia."

Essence fluttered her eyelashes as if she were insulted. She pulled on my free arm roughly. "Don't you walk away from me. I deserve an explanation."

"I don't owe you anything, Essence. You broke our bond and even then, I've been trying to make this work between us, but it's not going to work."

"You did this to me and now you expect me to go on with my life?"

"This was a decision you made."

"Wrong! You made that decision for me."

The angrier she got, the louder her voice became.

Olivia pulled my hand gently. "Rain, your mother is waiting to talk to you. I'll come with you if you want me to."

Essence threw her head back and laughed hysterically. "You're such a puppet, Rain. You do everything your mommy tells you to do. I'm your wife and I say we're leaving this party now."

I turned around and glared at her. I was on the verge of putting her in her place until Olivia pulled my hand again.

"Come on, Rain. Walk away."

"I'm talking to him!" Essence exploded so loudly that the whole floor shook.

Azura hissed, Legend balled up his fists, and Onyx stood to his feet. Essence's lip curled into a devious smile. She looked as if she were ready to take us all on if she had to. I held up my hand to alert them to be still.

As I walked away toward the library, I said, "Essence, you can see yourself out."

She jumped on my back, grabbing me tightly around my neck as she wrapped her legs around my waist. I tried to get her off, but her grip became too tight. She put up a good fight, but I was stronger. I struggled to pull her off. Her claw-like nails were digging into my neck as she ripped my shirt. I felt the burn as I pushed her as hard as I could, which caused her to fly back against the wall. The brick shattered.

She eased off the ground and laughed in a shrill manner. She snatched my father's sword off the mantel and charged at me. Before I could get out of her way, she stabbed me with it. I doubled over as my blood gushed out of me. Onyx, Legend, and Azura took hold of her. When Essence realized they were too strong for her, she broke through the pristine glass window and disappeared.

I pulled the sword out and the wound started healing immediately. I made my way to the library quickly. Everyone followed behind me.

"Rain, are you all right?" Chantal asked, trying to see if I was still bleeding.

"I'm fine. It's healing."

"What's wrong with her?" Olivia asked.

"Don't worry about her."

As soon as I entered into the library, I could see Mother's and Father's grim faces.

"Do you see what you've done," Mother said. "That woman has crossed over, Rain. There's no getting her back. Let her be. She is now the enemy."

"Mother, let me handle this."

"Be aware. The power that she has is one that we will all have to come together to destroy. You, alone, won't be able to kill her," she replied.

"I created her, so I will end this. No one is to lay a finger on her. Leave that up to me."

They all paid very close attention to the tone of my voice. They had never heard this tone from me. It was the tone of their leader.

After the gathering, everyone went home. I wasn't going to go home; the wild banshee was waiting for me to return. She could've easily made her way back to my parents' house, but she wanted to catch me alone. I wasn't going to let her have her way.

Olivia stayed with me in the living room by the grand fireplace.

"You should really come to New Orleans sometime to get away from this mess," Olivia said, trying to lighten up my sullen mood.

"That would be nice." I headed straight to the liquor cabinet, poured some rum and downed the drink. I needed it.

Olivia stared at me with those blue eyes penetrating mine. She positioned her body right up against me. "Rain, do you think about getting back together?"

"Olivia, what we shared was precious and we shared some of the best times of my life. I'll always cherish those memories. I missed you and anything is possible in the future. It's that right now, I need a little time to get myself together."

"You're in love with her."

"Yes."

"You always love too hard."

"There's no such thing. Well, at least, not in my book."

"Are you afraid that she will try to hurt you?"

"I don't fear her. Are you afraid that she'll hurt me?"

She dropped her teary eyes from mine. "No, I just want to be with you."

"Being with me is too complicated and I don't want to break your heart. This may sound foolish, but until I resolve things with Essence, I can never give myself to you completely. Every time I start to fall for a woman, she breaks my spirit."

She bit on her lower lip. "I will never break your spirit again."

"Once is all it takes. It will be hard for you to undo what you've already done."

"Will it?"

Her blue eyes had me staring too deeply. Suddenly, I grabbed the back of her head with two hands, pulled her to me, and kissed her passionately. When she expressed her love for me, I didn't want to deny it. Felt too good to deny it. Was it too soon to let her back in?

Our tongues danced sweetly, melodically to our own rhythm. I'd forgiven her a long time ago for hurting me by leaving for so long.

"If you want me, Rain, take me. I want to be yours."

I gave her neck a sensual nibble. In the heat of our passion, I wanted to make love to her for the rest of the night.

"The only way you can have me back is if you get rid of *her*."

"What?" I asked, coming out of my lust-filled daze.

There was no need to discuss Essence. She should've been the last person on her mind. I should've been the only one on her mind. I was about to give her an experience only I could give.

"I love you so much, Rain. I don't know what to do with myself. All I do is think of you, night after night, day after day. I really missed you."

I pulled her body against mine roughly. After easing all her clothes off in a hurried fashion, we were making out as if it would be our last time feeling one another. Our breaths became one as I used just the tip of me to play with her slick opening.

"I've wanted to feel you for so long."

Placing my finger over her lips to hush her, I smothered her lips with a deep kiss. In and out of her, I pumped thoroughly. Our rigid grinds took us away until the early hours of the wee morning.

CHAPTER 26

ONYX

Five months later…

O nce Soleil was completely naked, she helped me get out of my clothes. She traced small circles along my chest hairs with the tips of her fingers as we lay in bed. I caressed her large tummy. I was so excited about the baby and he was going to be coming soon. She felt a sharp pain and she clutched her stomach.

"Looks like our miracle is coming, Onyx. My water just broke."

Soleil wanted the birth of our child to be private, between the two of us, but that was close to impossible while giving birth in my family's mansion. Twenty-two hours of labor and I felt as if I had just given birth myself. That's how exhausted I was. As soon as our son was born, Mother and Father wanted him in their arms to hold. My premonition of a son had come true. I had been right. They were the proudest days of my life.

We named him Ulysses like the title of the novel written by the Irish writer James Joyce. Ulysses was the hero in Homer's poem "Odyssey." He was also the Greek leader that came up with the plan to burn down Troy and save Helen during the Trojan War. I loved everything there was to know about Greek mythology and Soleil thought the name was perfect for him.

Everyone from our family was there to witness his birth and every-one was as happy as we were. There was no talk of the Préfet. They weren't aware of what was going on. Our parents' plan had worked better than we'd imagined.

The baby had his eyes opened for his grandparents. He sucked his fingers, wiggling into a cry.

"Uh-oh, Mommy," Mother said. "Baby is hungry."

He cried and Soleil became alert instantly as if her mother radar had kicked in already. She positioned herself wearily. I helped her by positioning a pillow underneath our son for her to breast-feed him.

"He's so perfect," Mother said with tears in her eyes.

"Yes, he sure is," I stated proudly.

"This calls for a toast," Azura said as she handed us glasses full of rose-colored champagne. "Rain, you should do the honors."

Everyone lifted their glasses after Rain.

He said, "While thus we agree, our toast let it be. May our little one flourish happy, united, and free? Long may the son of Onyx and Soleil entwine the myrtle of Venus with Bacchus's vine! Ulysses."

We all laughed at his humor of combining the old Greek drink-ing song into his toast as we drank in celebration of the birth of a vampire. Ulysses was pureblooded and it was no myth.

CHAPTER 27

LEGEND

By the time I made it home from the birth of Ulysses, Chantal wasn't home. I called her cell phone, but she didn't answer. I turned on the laptop while sitting on the couch to view my e-mails. A few bank statements alerted me that a few purchases went through that morning. Chantal knew how to spend a whole shitload of money. Even though I was smart enough to have daily cash withdrawal limits, Chantal swiped that card any- and everywhere she went. She shopped for the most expensive things she could find and it was becoming ridiculous.

What in hell did she want with Versace China?

There was a knock on the front door. I answered it to find a mortal in his early thirties.

"Is Chantal here?" he asked with a frown.

"You have the wrong address."

"Chantal doesn't live here?"

"She sure doesn't."

"Look, she's been staying here. She gave me this address to come for her. I'm her husband and I'm here to take her home."

"Is that so?"

"Yeah, that's so."

"All right, well, come in and have a seat. She should be here in a moment."

I let him in and walked down the hallway. She had the nerve to tell him to come pick her up when I had specifically given her direct instructions. My thought was to take a huge bite out of him and drink every ounce of blood he had in his body, but then I stopped myself. If he was whom she wanted, then I was going to allow her to have her wish.

"Have a seat. Would you like a beverage of some sort?" I offered.

He stared at me oddly, guarded, and refused to sit on the couch. I knew then that he knew more than he should've. He was a brave soul to come to the door of a vampire's home.

"No, I'm fine. Do you know when she'll be here?"

"She didn't tell me she was leaving."

"Well, I'll come back a little later on. She should be ready by the time I come back."

"Ready for what?"

He swallowed hard as if a lump had formed in his throat. "She should be ready to leave with me."

"Oh…okay…sure…"

He turned and walked out the door. I closed it behind him and went to stand on the balcony, in the dark and cold. I didn't feel as if her husband was any type of dangerous threat. I didn't know anything about him, but I could smell his fear. Fear was the most dangerous type of weapon. Fear would make a man kill even if he had never thought of killing before.

I heard her come in the door twenty minutes later. She was talking on the phone, laughing with shopping bags in each hand. Seemed like she was having a ball all on me, at my expense.

Chantal didn't see me because I was sitting underneath the shadows outside on the balcony. Someone must've called her other line. She said, "Hold on a second… Hello… Hey, baby. What's up?"

The sound of the excitement in her voice when she talked to him made my nose flare. She was glad he called. "What?" She gasped and then paused as if paralyzed. "You did? Um, I don't know… Look, I'll call you right back." She wore a look of terror as her body stiffened.

She straightened up, placing the bags on the floor. "Legend! I'm home!" she yelled, walking briskly to the kitchen. Her heels clicked against the wood floors.

I entered silently and sat on the couch.

As soon as she reentered the living room, she saw me. "Hey… Legend."

I clenched my teeth to stop myself from calling Chantal out of her name. "Your real husband came by looking for you."

"I know." Her brown eyes, the same eyes that looked at me with sincerity when she told me she loved me, were full of deceit, lies, and betrayal. "I can explain everything." Tears fell from her eyes.

"You don't have to explain anything to me. You are officially free to leave. Truth of the matter, you could've left a long time ago, but you chose this life and you chose to stay. Does he know that you're no longer a human being?"

"Yes," she admitted. "And he doesn't care. He just wants me to come home."

"How do the two of you plan on living that way?"

"I don't know. All I know is that I miss him." She was worried that it wasn't going to work out with him, but she was willing to give it a shot.

"Why were you here in Paris pretending to be a single woman? Why did you come to the Red Light District?"

"We were having problems and I wanted to have a good time. I didn't plan on any of this."

"If you would've told me, I would've never sunk my fangs into you. Why'd you lie?"

"I don't know…I was in vacation mode. I was playing this game to piss him off, at first. Look, Legend, I thank you for turning me into such a beautiful immortal, and I love staying this way, but I don't want to stay with you."

"Oh yeah? Well, here's your wakeup call, sweetie. You'll never be able to leave Pigalle Palace with that human being alive. Do you understand me?"

"Who's going to kill me? You?"

I shook my head. "No. The Préfet take matters like these into their own hands. The moment you walk out that door with him, you'll never make it to the airport. Trust me when I say that."

Unfazed by what I was saying, she looked at her cell phone that buzzed. "He's downstairs waiting for me. I guess this is goodbye."

She quickly reached into her purse and returned my debit card along with the diamond ring. She turned and walked out the door.

CHAPTER 28

AZURA

I usually held private parties at either my house or upstairs of the club. I liked to invite what we called the VIP upstairs for some fun. I had never tried, or been particularly interested in, threesomes with only women. I usually preferred orgies with a few men and a few women, but it was one of those things I had to try to gain a new experience.

I always had an attraction to women, something I liked to hide from my family because they were too judgmental. Since my brothers were preoccupied with their own women issues, I decided to take full advantage of my alone time in the club without them.

The good thing that I enjoyed about threesomes was that there was double the pleasure. Sometimes, someone felt left out, but I always did my absolute best to keep everyone engaged. My encounter that night was one I would never forget.

She was tall, with blonde hair and crystal-blue eyes. She was very slender and she had a real sultry look; as if she were a dancer.

"Are you a stripper?" I asked when she paid at the door.

"I dance at a club around the corner," she admitted.

Even after she walked away to party with friends, she had been staring me down all night, as if she wanted to have me all to herself. At first, I tried not to notice, but then it became hard for me not to observe.

She nearly intimidated me. She wasn't the kind of woman that looked at me and then turned away. She stared me directly in my eye and winked. She had this look on her face like she wanted to rip all my clothes apart. That's how intense she was.

There was another girl in the club, but she was there with a male. Maybe he was her friend; I wasn't sure. I'd seen her around the club a few times, but never with the same group of people. She would always gaze at me whenever she came. At first, I thought that she was staring at Onyx, so I ignored her.

When I realized she was staring at me, I started looking at her, too. By that time, she was dancing all over her male friend with his hands climbing up her skirt. She was tall with red hair, dark eyes, and darker skin. She had a little body fat and it was exactly where she needed it. Her thickness was sexy to me. Her face was really pretty.

I was still collecting money at door, when I saw the redhead helping her friend sit on one of our lounge couches. He was wasted. We made eye contact for a while and she smiled at me. I returned it. I sat there while she walked over to me.

She said, "*Bonjour*, beautiful. I'm Eve. What's your name?"

"My name is Azura."

We shook hands and I could feel an electric spark between us. Her hand was so soft that I never wanted to let go. We held each other's hand for a split-second longer than necessary, then I said, "I see you around here a lot. Are you enjoying yourself tonight?"

"My friends and I love this place." She took notice of the blonde watching our interaction very carefully. "The blonde is sexy."

She looked at me to see my reaction, and I replied, "Yeah, she is. Many guys fantasize about her...and some women, too. I mean, I would imagine so."

Her laugh was cute when she said, "I bet you're one of those women, aren't you?"

I answered truthfully, "She's a nice one to fantasize about."

Her eyebrow rose. "I agree. Anyone else you fantasize about in here?"

Eve knew exactly where she wanted this to go. I grinned at her. "Wouldn't you like to know?"

"Why don't we go somewhere private so you can tell me? I hear there are private rooms upstairs. Then, nobody will overhear you," she said, as if somebody overhearing me was what I was worried about.

"What about your friend?"

"He's drunk. Someone will make sure he gets home."

"All right, let's go."

We left the strobe lights and noise of the club, and she followed me upstairs to the largest room we had. There were toys, hand-cuffs, whips, chains, and all types of dominant toys in that room. I only liked to use those when I was role-playing.

She sat on the couch that was in the corner of the room. "So are you ever gonna tell me about these fantasies?"

I felt my nipples harden. "I think you can pretty much imagine all the possibilities."

"Tell me what kind of woman you're attracted to."

"Well...I like a woman with long, straight, red hair...really dark eyes...and a big ass."

She smiled triumphantly. "I thought so. Want to know what kind of woman I like?"

"Tell me."

She said, "Light-almond-shaped eyes, a bright smile, and juicy-looking lips."

"Oh, would that be me?"

"That would be you, Azura."

Eve stood in front of me and leaned down to kiss me. She held my face with both hands and her tongue slipped into my mouth. My hands went to her hips and pulled her in closer. She managed to straddle my lap. Our kiss got deeper and more passionate. My panties started getting wet and my whole world felt like it was in her body.

Her hands continued to caress my face and hair, rubbing my shoulders occasionally. We made little moans into each other's mouths. My hands moved down to massage her thick ass. I slid one hand under her shirt and bra, feeling her breast directly against my hand. I squeezed lightly and rubbed my thumb over her quickly hardening nipple. Her body jerked when I touched her nipple and she moaned louder. I bit her bottom lip as I pressed her nipple into her breast, and then rolled it between two fingers.

We both heard the door open. She jerked again, but this time in surprise. Eve remained on my lap. I looked up and saw the blonde. She must've followed us. She was standing directly in front of us, and neither of us moved.

Eve was the first to say something. "Well, look who decided to join the party."

The blonde girl, whose name I later found out was Tiffany, looked at me and said, "So, you're a lesbian. Good. I was starting to think my senses were off."

"Your senses are on point, tonight."

Tiffany said, "Good." Then, she hesitated before she asked, "Would you mind if I joined you ladies?"

I was thinking this couldn't have happened more perfectly. I came to work expecting to spend my evening fucking a man of my choice, but ended up with two women in my room. This had never happened to me while at Vaisseau and trust, many freaky things happened over the years.

Eve said, "I wouldn't mind, would you, Azura?"

"I don't mind at all. Make yourself comfortable."

She sat next to us. Eve proceeded with kissing me. Tiffany watched us for a few minutes. Then, she started taking off her clothes. I put my hand on Tiffany's breasts to get her involved. She moaned.

Eve noticed Tiffany was naked, so she took her clothes off, too. I stared at their beautiful bodies, two shades of light and dark next to one another. I stood and they undressed me next.

They seemed to like what they saw because they both had looks of pleasure all over their faces. Tiffany kissed me deeply, holding me close to her. Eve came up behind me and kissed my neck, putting her arms around both of us while pressing against me.

This was something I'd never experienced before, two women kissing me at once. It felt amazing.

Tiffany started massaging Eve's ass, and Eve moaned into my neck as she rubbed the inside of my thighs from behind. I moaned into Tiffany's mouth and pushed my hips forward into her hips, causing our pussies to press against each other. Both of us were shaved, and it felt so smooth when our pussies rubbed against each other.

I wondered what Eve was doing because I was lost in Tiffany's kiss, but Eve had managed to grab a dildo from the display case. Tiffany led me to the bed where she placed her body underneath mine. Eve got on her knees on the bed and rubbed the tip of the toy against my clit. I felt so much pleasure.

I moaned loudly into Tiffany's mouth and she took my breasts in her hands and massaged them, then sucked on one nipple while she pinched the other. This was a sensory overload for me and I actually came right then.

The other two girls seemed to take my orgasm in stride while Tiffany moved lower so that I could ride her face. She licked my slit from back to front. Eve held onto me from behind while she massaged my breasts. When I was done coming on Tiffany's face, I eased off.

Eve and Tiffany licked each other's tongues. Eve bent me over and pulled my cheeks apart. She inserted the toy into me. When she thrust her hips, that's when I learned that she had the toy on. Tiffany started rapidly flicking the tip of her tongue on my breasts. It felt incredible to have someone fuck me while someone else was sucking my nipple; this was almost too much to handle.

It didn't take me long to come again, and while I was coming down from my orgasm, Tiffany kissed Eve, sharing my juices with her. It was a pleasant contrast, one blonde and one redhead. They started fondling each other's breasts. Eve stood up so her pussy was in Tiffany's face. Tiffany started eating Eve, tonguing her hole, then moving up and flicking her tongue against Eve's clit as she did mine.

I went over to Tiffany and placed my head between her legs. Tiffany noticed what I was doing and lowered herself down onto my face. This was when I realized that Tiffany was pierced.

Eve was moaning above me from the pleasure Tiffany was giving her. My tongue lapped the bar in Tiffany's clit, playing with it and pushing it around. Tiffany moaned loudly into Eve's pussy, which made Eve moan again. I could see Eve's breasts from underneath Tiffany and Tiffany's face buried in Eve's pussy.

I made Tiffany cum. Her thighs shook around my head and she screamed into Eve's pussy. I licked up the remaining moisture around her thighs, and then untangled myself from Tiffany's legs. As I was doing that, Eve started coming, and Tiffany stuck a finger inside of her. This drove Eve over the edge.

Once Eve came, we shared a three-way kiss. Eve rubbed my clit. Eve broke the kiss and Tiffany sat back, watching. I leaned back on my arms, and Tiffany reached over and played with my breasts.

Right then, there was a knock on the door, which startled all of us. Legend yelled through the door, "Azura, everyone is leaving. Lock up when you leave."

"All right."

We started giggling.

I looked at them and said, "Now, where were we?"

CHAPTER 29

RAIN

Things had been quiet. Essence hadn't surprised me with her presence since she'd made that big scene at my parents'. I had a hard time getting Olivia to leave my side; she wanted to stay with me. I didn't refuse her. Her company was actually soothing.

The house phone was ringing close to four in the morning. I reached over since Olivia had just started to fall asleep. I got off work early and we made love hard. I made her cum five to six times, peaking and exploding into multiple orgasms. She had the trembles so bad that simply the touch of my hands made her go back into convulsions. Sleep soon followed.

"Hello..."

"Rain," Mother cried on the other end of the phone.

I sat straight up. "What's the matter?"

She cried harder into the phone. "The Préfet... They came and took the baby."

"When?"

"They took the baby about twenty minutes ago. They're going to expose him to the sun at dawn, Rain. We all have to be there to stand trial..."

"I'm on my way. Where's Onyx and Soleil?"

"They were taken with him...to a cell. Hurry." She hung up.

I didn't hesitate before I got out of bed and changed out of my bedclothes. I didn't want to wake Olivia, so I left her sleeping soundly.

I got to my mother's house as fast as I could.

"How did they find out?" I demanded.

Mother was crying uncontrollably.

Legend replied, "They know everything and they've known for some time. They were just waiting… They killed Chantal and her husband before they could make it to the airport."

"When?"

"A few hours ago. Court will be held in an hour, and at dawn they will open the roof and the sun will hit Ulysses' skin."

I placed my hand on the top of Mother's hair. "Mother, look at me, please."

She lifted her head slowly. Her eyes were swollen and bloodshot.

I took a deep breath and exhaled, feeling like I was the only one that could save us all from the ill fate of the Préfet. "Don't cry. Nobody should be crying right now. We've been waiting our whole lives for this moment. This is the moment that we find out if the Divination is in fact true."

"Rain, you don't know that! You haven't been in the sun since you changed!" Father fired my way. "What if Ulysses dies? Our miracle will be gone just like that and they will kill the rest of us."

"He's not going to die. We're not going to die. I promise you that."

I had a plan and my family was going to have to trust me on this. I didn't know if I could stand one ray of sun, but I felt that something bigger was about to happen.

As soon as we entered the Château de Chambord, we didn't utter a single word. Azura, Legend, Mother, Father, and I held our heads high. We didn't have to be ashamed. Though it felt like Doomsday, we were going to be able to prove the Divination true.

The Château de Chambord had been taken over by the Préfet when abandoned in 1883 when King Allemand was murdered. The killer was burned at the stake for high treason and no other King had sat on that throne.

It was a beautiful castle with a keep and corner towers, and was defended by a large moat. Built in Renaissance style, the internal layout was an early example of how the French and Italian style would group rooms into self-contained suites. The medieval-styled corridor rooms were breathtaking. The massive château was composed of a central keep with four immense bastion towers at the four corners. The keep also formed a part of the front wall of a larger compound with two more large towers. Bases for a possible further two towers were found at the rear, but these were never developed, and remained the same height as the wall. The château featured 440 rooms, 282 fireplaces, eighty-four staircases, and four rectangular vaulted hallways on each floor formed a cross-shape.

The Préfet was going to turn the castle over to the new King.

A line of officers led us to a dim candlelit courtroom. There was no surprise that the court was filled with over eighty elder vampires from our community, all wanting to witness the outcome.

When I looked at the fear in my family's eyes, I felt something in the pit of my stomach. It caused my mind to race. How was I going to get us out of this mess alive? I never wanted to see fear on my family's faces ever again. I clenched my teeth to keep my anger under control.

I turned my head to the right: *she* was there. I could smell *her*. Essence was in the courtroom, but I couldn't spot her.

Legend, Azura, Mother, Father, and I were seated on a bench

that was guarded by armed officers. We waited patiently to see if Onyx and Soleil would be allowed to come into court.

The Chancellor was Keeper of the Seal and he was in charge of officiating justice. He and his officials had been waiting for our arrival.

"Everyone is now here... Bring them in," he said in a calm manner.

Soleil's and Onyx's feet and hands were chained together as they filed into the courtroom led by an officer. As they stood in front of us, I noticed the bruises and whip marks through their torn clothes. Blood coming from their wounds made me ball up my fists. They weren't healing as fast as usual and that made me believe they were given a serum to weaken them. They had been tortured for an answer, but they had no answers.

Only I had the answers. It was time to show them what I knew.

"I see the Toussaint family is all here minus Legend's fraudulent wife. She's been taken care of..." The Chancellor nodded his head at one of the officers.

An officer announced, "Court is now in session."

"We are here on the matters of the Toussaint family. You have managed to hide the pregnancy of Onyx's wife, Soleil. Once the baby was born, you still didn't report the birth. Why was that?"

Father stood to talk, but before he could get a word in, the Chancellor signaled for him to sit down.

"I want to hear from the divine one...Rain."

I stood with my head held high. "Yes, Chancellor."

"Why didn't you or anyone in your family report the birth of this vampire child?"

"We wanted to make sure that the child was safe and we wanted to see for ourselves if in fact he was a Daywalker."

The crowd gasped and small chatter proceeded.

The Chancellor yelled, "Order…*Arrêté*…"

The chatter stopped.

He continued, "Were you able to test this theory?"

"Not yet."

"Have you, yourself, been out in the sun yet?" the Chancellor asked with wide curious eyes.

"…Not yet, Chancellor."

"Why is that? Do you not believe in the Divination?"

"It's not that I don't believe in it… I'm not ready…"

"You're not ready to be King? That's assuming you are truly who your family thinks you are…" The Chancellor gave a head nod to one of the officers.

The officers grabbed me roughly and bound me down to the ground underneath the sunroof with steel chains. I didn't put up a fight. I wouldn't have been able to win. There were too many of them.

"No!" Mother shouted.

Father held her while chatter filled the room.

"*Arrêté!*"

The court was quiet again.

"Bring out the baby!" the Chancellor demanded.

The baby was held by an officer. He was sleeping soundly. We could tell Ulysses was still alive because he started to stir once they laid him next to me. When I looked over at him, he actually turned to stare at me. My nephew was a wonderful gift and one of us was going to change our world.

"In less than five minutes, the sunroof will open and the sun will beam down on this area only. If the Divination has been interpreted correctly, only one of you will burn. Which one will it be? If we have misinterpreted the Divination, then you both will burn to death." The Chancellor was firm in his decision. "Does anyone in this courtroom, other than the ones standing trial, feel this is unjust?"

The courtroom was still and no one spoke up. I could hear sobs from my family, but I kept my eyes on the baby. One of us wasn't going to burn; I wasn't sure which one of us was going to die.

"If they both burn, the family will be burned for misleading the government into thinking that this is the next royal family. If one of them survives the sun, then you will live and will be set free."

The sound of the sunroof starting to move rumbled like thunder.

"It's time. The moment of truth is here…" the Chancellor said.

Everyone watched and I held my breath as tears emerged. I kept my gaze on Ulysses. He was so innocent and unaware of what was happening. If he lived through this, he would be able to tell this story.

As the sun started coming in slowly, it started at the top of my head. The bright light hurt my eyes, so I closed them, but I wanted to see the baby, so I turned my head to rest against the concrete. Surprisingly, the sun was not burning my skin. The sun wasn't burning me. That had to mean that Ulysses was going to turn to ash. I panicked as I kept my eyes on him. As soon as the sun touched the top of his head, I cringed. The sun moved down to his eyebrows, and that's when I realized what was happening.

Not only was the sun shining brightly on his entire body, he started glowing. What did the glow mean? Was I glowing, too? I looked at my hands. I didn't have the same glow. Why was he glowing?

The whole court exploded in loud chatter.

"*Un miracle!*"

"*Incroyable!*"

"*Phénoménal!*"

"*Vive le roi et le prince!*"

The Chancellor stood in disbelief and allowed the court's commotion to continue until the sunroof had fully opened. The sun was beaming and we were not burned. He finally hit his gavel against the table. "Close the roof and unchain him!"

The roof closed and I was set free. I picked up Ulysses, who was staring directly at me with a smile. I smiled back at him. Not only was the Divination proved true that day, it came with another surprise. There were two future kings in their presence.

The Chancellor bowed and the officials stood and then bowed as well.

"King Rain and Prince Ulysses... We've waited a long time for you."

CHAPTER 30

RAIN

Ulysses and I were Daywalkers, and together, we were going to put order back into the lives of our community. I was glad there was some peace in our lives again. I had some business I had to conduct with another official in Versailles who wanted to hold a crowning ceremony. He suggested that the family sell Club Vaisseau and move into Château de Chambord as quickly as possible to start my duties as the King of Pigalle Palace.

Azura was the only one who wanted to keep the club. She wasn't ready to trade in her miniskirt for a gown, so I was going to try my best to talk them into letting her keep it. I couldn't be anywhere near the club. There would have to be a level of protection to surround me while out in public places.

I checked into a hotel in Versailles that night.

Once in the lobby, I thought I caught a glimpse of Essence, but I wasn't sure. She looked so different, but her scent was the same. I could always smell her. Was she following me? I didn't know if I should've headed for the door. Instead, I stood at the front of the lobby, watching her every move.

She must've felt my eyes when she turned her head toward my direction. When she saw me, she disappeared behind a column. I dashed her way, but she was gone.

Once I was in the hotel's room on the top floor, I opened the balcony, and sat in a chair. I lit a complimentary cigar and waited for Essence. I could feel her. She was near. She still smelled like the delicate flower that I loved so much. The moment she flew inside, I smiled on the inside. She had become too predictable, but that's what I liked most about our nexus.

"When will you get tired of playing hide-and-go-seek with me?" I asked.

A slight smile graced her beautiful face. I could read her mind because she hadn't learned how to block me out of her head yet. She was wondering whom I loved and fucked while she had been away. That was the only thing on her mind and that made me chuckle to myself.

Suddenly, she thought about leaving. It was no fun to pursue me when I was expecting her. When she turned to leave, I stopped her.

"Are you having second thoughts now that you're here?" I blew out smoke.

"No," she lied.

"Leaving so soon?"

She faced me again and replied, "How did you know I was coming up here?"

"Why are you following me?"

"Because this desire I have for you won't go away."

I shouldn't have had any feelings for Essence anymore, but releasing some tension sexually deep into her was something I couldn't stop thinking about. Seeing Essence like this was bad, but at that moment, I didn't care about anything else but making her scream my name.

"I acknowledge our tension, but I really think you came here to hurt me or try."

I put out the cigar and invaded her personal space. I inhaled her from where I was standing. She bared her fangs before she licked her lips seductively. Her wild, jet-black hair formed into a wavy afro. It was becoming, but it made her look like the wild banshee that she had adopted.

"In Montmartre…nearly seven months ago, Rain, you bit me…"

"Essence, why'd you come up here tonight? What is it about me that has you refusing to be without me?"

"Shhhh," she hushed me before wrapping her arms around my neck. She pulled my hands to her ass. I squeezed her as we danced slowly in a small circle as if there was music playing.

I hated to admit that I missed my ex-wife. I wished I was over Essence, but I wasn't, not even a little bit. The dreams I had been having about her wouldn't stop. She had been manipulating my dreams and I didn't care. I enjoyed them.

When I lay next to Olivia, I thought of Essence. It wasn't right, but it was the truth.

I removed Essence's shirt without her permission to reveal her breasts. She wasn't wearing a bra. I kissed and nibbled her nipples, making my tongue dance on them until they got hard. She pushed me back to relax on the couch and unbuckled my pants. Within seconds, she sat on my hardness.

On top of me, she was riding me so good that all I could do was exhale.

"I missed kissing you… I missed loving you… I missed fucking you… I missed this… I missed you," she moaned, and with each word, my dick got harder.

I pulled her off me and pushed her on the floor to get on all fours.

"Do you miss me because I'm King?"

"You're not the King, yet, baby."

"I am."

"Where's your crown?"

I thrust into her as hard as I could and that made her shut up her crazy talk. I made her cum repeatedly until we shared the last orgasm. All of the tension she had in her body was released and she relaxed in my arms. I propped my elbow on the carpet and rested my head in my hand to stare into her eyes.

Essence stared at me with her eyes watering a little. "I can't stay mad at you for long, Rain, but I see you are with Olivia now. How can you move on this way without me?"

"Easy. You broke our bond," I replied and then rested my head into the valley between her supple breasts.

She caressed the top of my head and I closed my eyes, feeling as if I never wanted to let her out of my arms. At that moment, I wished the feeling would never go away. She needed to be with me. The path she had chosen wasn't what I had in mind for her. Essence was beginning to destruct anything in her path with her brood. I didn't want her to be the Queen of the Darkness. I wanted her to be the Queen of Pigalle Palace.

"What would Olivia think?" she asked, reading my thoughts.

I smiled on the inside because she had been given my power of mind reading.

"Don't bring Olivia into this."

"I wouldn't have to if you would leave her and be with me."

I refused to answer her.

"Why else would you leave the balcony open for me? I'll tell you why. It's because you still want me. So, let's get to why I'm here. I need you, Rain. Your power with mine, we could do so many great things together. My brood is growing."

"I heard about your so-called brood. Honestly, your brood is nothing but a bunch of blood-sucking demons."

"I didn't come up here for the guilt trip. I saw you and your nephew, Ulysses, in court. Quite admirable and impressive. This city will have two Daywalkers... Kings... I can only imagine how jealous that makes some feel."

"There's no jealousy. The people are overjoyed to have a leader. They hate the government. Look, I know why you came here. You wanted to try to kill me; instead, I wound up fucking you senseless." I removed myself from her body. "You do know that you won't be able to kill me, right?"

"And you don't have the nerve to kill me."

"So, let's agree to disagree."

"That's fine with me."

"You move your brood away from Pigalle Palace immediately. I will be crowned in a few days. The Préfet is stepping down and their only job will be to hold court. As long as you're away, I won't seek you out. Oh, and quit trying to manipulate my dreams."

She drifted off into thought for a split-second. "Rain, you know that you enjoy me in your dreams."

"I enjoy you in and out of my dreams."

"You're such a good man. It's a shame you don't know anything about being faithful."

"I am faithful."

"You were faithful before tonight." She loved to push my buttons—always did.

I tried to put my clothes on, but she pulled on my arm.

"I'm sorry, Rain. I'm having some fun with you. I don't want you to kick me out yet."

"You want to torture me and make me feel bad about fucking you."

"I promise you...I won't say another word about this."

"Good."

"Lay with me. Feels like old times..."

I didn't want her to leave, either and it did feel like old times.

CHAPTER 31

RAIN

When I got home from Versailles, I could hear the shower in my master bathroom running. I went into the steamy bathroom. Her body, silhouetted from the door of the marbled steam unit, had me fixated. I watched her shadow move around underneath the hot water as she bathed.

I smiled to myself, wondering if she knew I was watching her. I wanted to rub her thighs, kiss her neck, and touch her hot spot until she came… Olivia.

I opened the door of the unit with a smile on my face. "Liv," I said with my eyebrows raised. "You've been waiting for me long?"

She took hold of my boxers with her warm wet hands. "I just got here. Get in with me."

I gently pulled away from her. "I wish I could play with you. I'm leaving on royal business in a bit. I can't be late."

She reached for a towel to wrap around her. "Can I come?"

"It's boring and long. You really want to come?"

"Where?"

"Up North."

"That sounds good to me."

"You sure you want to roll with me on business? I'm traveling in the day."

She groaned, "Aw, I really want to, but the sun will be too much; then maybe I should stay here."

"I don't care if you come, really." I kissed her on her damp fore-head.

She smiled. I stared at the water beads completely covering her body. Her hair had gotten moist while in the shower. She fluttered her eyelashes up at me because she was watching me gawk at her nakedness.

"What?" I asked.

"What you think about when you stare at me like that?"

"A lot of things."

"Like?" she pressed.

"Well, Olivia. I wonder if I am the man that can truly keep you happy. I couldn't keep Essence happy."

She rolled her eyes. "I really want you to move on from her. When you dream, you talk in your sleep. I'm truly tired of hearing her name."

"I don't say her name in my sleep."

She frowned as if I had said something crazy. "Night after night, you moan her name."

The dreams I'd had about Essence felt real. I dazed off thinking about them.

"You saw her, didn't you?" Olivia asked, interrupting my thoughts.

"Why you ask me that?"

She laughed a little as if I were silly. "You're joking, right?"

"What?"

"You saw her!"

"Look, Olivia, I'm trying to move on and get her out of my system."

"No, you're not. What is it about that woman? I'm standing in your bathroom, naked. I can't get you to stop thinking about her. She's like poison. Her intentions aren't good, Rain. Can't you see that?"

"Liv, I have to get dressed, so if you're going with me, hurry up. I need to get in the shower, too."

She hopped back in the shower to finish her bath. "Don't do this to me, Rain. I want you to stay focused."

I smiled to myself. I had plans for Olivia. She didn't know it yet. I was waiting for the perfect moment.

Her blue eyes stared through me once she was done showering.

Guilt set in like a motherfucker. I was a fool. I was so deep into Essence's games that I was falling right into the palm of her hand. I was very aware of it.

We embraced.

She took hold of my hand and guided it between her legs. "Look at what you do to me."

I licked my lips and smiled at her. "As much as I would love to play with you, we have somewhere to be."

She nodded. "To be continued."

"Definitely."

CHAPTER 32

ONYX

"Why is the baby crying like that?" I asked while entering Ulysses' nursery.

"Because I'm changing his stinky little diaper and he doesn't like it."

"I see that. You're such a good mother, Soleil."

She grinned from ear to ear. "He's such a good little baby. When will everything be finalized for the move into the Chateau?"

"Next week."

"Great. You know how badly we need daddy around here... How's everything else going?"

"Good. Rain is finishing some more business. Legend is working closely with our parents to make sure our move will go smoothly."

"I still can't believe we will be moving into the castle."

"Everything feels so surreal. I look forward to watching Ulysses grow into the kind of man he's destined to be. Rain is going to make an excellent King."

"I agree... Do you think he'll make Olivia his Queen?"

"Seems that way, but lately, he's been sort of distant about his love life. I think all of this royalty business is putting him in a different mind frame."

"True."

"I saw Essence in court."

"I saw her, too. She was wearing that hooded cloak, but I noticed her."

"Do you think she wants to be back with Rain?"

"Of course she does. Why wouldn't she? That would make her Queen."

Soleil shook her head. "Essence as the Queen of Pigalle… I would hate to be under her thumb."

CHAPTER 33

RAIN

For the next few days, Olivia and I traveled on royalty business. I shielded her from the sun with extra clothing and covering. We had to let all the mayors of the surrounding vampire cities know that The Préfet was stepping down from its position. I was welcomed warmly and I looked forward to the crowning ceremony.

While away, Essence entered my dreams again. She was trying to make me her sex slave. I allowed her to do so. She took her sweet time in each of them and she even spoke so loud and clear. I started taking control of these dreams. I tied her up, blindfolded her, and gave her sex exactly the way I did when we weren't dreaming.

When Olivia and I returned to Montmartre, I left her at home so I could meet the family at the mansion to discuss the final things that needed to be done before taking the throne. Fall had turned all of the leaves orange in my yard. I buttoned up my black pea coat and made my way through the piles of orange leaves before walking onto the pavement. The brisk air tickled my nose as I walked down the wet street to find a cab.

Before I could flag one down, Essence appeared behind me, but I couldn't see her when I turned around. I could only smell her.

She kept her distance as she followed me. I pretended as if I wasn't aware of her presence. She got too close. I turned around suddenly to face her. Her wide smile greeted me.

"When will you learn that I can always smell you before I see you?"

She giggled as her feet met the ground. "Did you miss me while you were away?"

"You can't keep following me like this. I told you to stay in your district."

"I know, but I can't resist. Did you dream about me?"

"You know good and well that I dreamed about you. Did you like the blindfold?"

"I loved the blindfold. We should try that sometime."

"These dreams are starting to get of control, don't you think?"

"Is that because you like them too much?" She wrapped her arms around my neck.

I didn't want to be seen, so I removed her hands. "Not out here."

"Your venom runs deep inside of me. I can't leave you alone. You know that."

"I won't talk out in the open this way."

Immediately, she pushed me into the alley we were passing, so we could be in the dark shadows. I let her pin me up against the building.

Her red eyes met mine through the dark. "Do you enjoy all of my stalking?" She ran her hand over my bulge.

"Of course I do."

"Yeah?"

"You really have to stop this, Essence." I tried to push her off with flat palms, but she planted her feet firmly, refusing to back away.

"You getting enough pussy from Olivia, or are you holding out for me?"

"Essence, don't…"

She bit on my lower lip as if she didn't hear what I said. I felt her sharp fangs, but she didn't pierce my skin. I clenched my jaws as she kissed me. Her lips were always so indulgent. I relaxed and let her tongue find its way inside my mouth to make circles around mine. Her aggressiveness was such a turn-on.

"Don't tell me you haven't thought about me outside of your dreams."

"I have...but..."

"But what? I know you're going to marry Olivia. She's sweet and pure, much like you wanted me to be. I can't stay away from you, Rain, and I know you feel the same about me. I'm hot for you like you are for me. Make me your Queen."

"I can't do that."

"Why can't you? You're going to be the King. You can do whatever you want to do. Mommy's and Daddy's opinions don't matter anymore. They will bow down to you now."

"Don't talk that way."

"Do you love Olivia?"

"I love her."

She threw her head back and laughed a little. "You're a liar. The way you look at me says something completely different. You mean to tell me you give it to Olivia the way you give it to me? Do you do that tornado thing with your tongue when you eat her pussy, too?"

"Stop it, Essence," I said, feeling frustrated with her antics.

"You know you don't give a shit about her... If you want me to back off, say it and you'll never hit this sweet pussy again."

She started unbuckling my pants. This could not be happening in the alley. She pulled my dick out and lifted up her dress. If this was what she wanted, then this was what she was going to get. I turned her around so she could face the wall of the building. I pushed her face against the wall and I entered inside of her.

Essence couldn't have been more right. Olivia didn't feel the way she did. Essence was the sexual beast I created. Her power over me was spreading and I was allowing it.

When I got home, it was early in the morning, around 5 a,m, Usually, Olivia was asleep, but she was still up, reading a book as she sat behind the UV-protected window. She was waiting for me. I had spent a few hours more than I wanted to with Essence. We had this heated session that ended with me fucking her until we both were exhausted. After sex, sex and more sex, our bodies were satisfying the urges that had us bound.

"Hey, what are you doing up? You should be enjoying your slumber right now."

"I can't sleep. Legend called earlier, but I'm sure he called your cell. You didn't make it to the family meeting?"

I swallowed hard and lied quickly, "I talked to him."

"Are you lying to me right now? Where have you been?"

"I had some other business to attend to and I didn't have time to make the meeting."

"I don't know if you know this, but I saw Essence following you when you left here. The last time I saw her, she was ready to kill you. She damned near tried to take your head off. So, how is it that you two can be so cordial?"

"Essence and I don't have any bad wishes upon one another."

"It's good to see you're so forgiving." Olivia's tone was icy enough to make me shiver.

I shook off her suspicion, standing in front of the bed with my pajama pants resting over my shoulder. "Are you bothered by this?"

"If you see *her* again, I can no longer be here with you."

"I understand."

She placed the book on her stomach. "Rain, the feelings you used to have for her are dead, right?"

"Of course."

I turned toward the bathroom, but she hopped off the bed and stood in front of me. "Rain, I'm not a complete fool. If you think for one second that I don't know what you and Essence have been up to, you're wrong. The only person you're truly hurting is...me. She's never going to stop trying to be in your life. You're making a fool of me and if you make her your Queen, your family will be disgraced."

She hit a nerve, but I kept my cool. "Don't speak on matters that don't concern you."

With tears in her eyes, she asked, "Do you even love me?"

Essence was like poison running through my veins, killing me slowly, but I stared into Olivia's eyes and said with conviction, "I love you."

Then, I quickly headed into the bathroom to get ready for bed before she could say another word.

CHAPTER 34

RAIN

"Is she the reason why you haven't left your house for days?" Essence questioned, jumping from a tree in front of Legend's home.

Legend and I were going to Onyx's home to see Ulysses. Our nephew needed to do some bonding with us. I was sick of Essence popping up wherever she wanted to. If the family knew how much time we had been spending together, they would be outraged. She was getting too close. Though her twisted obsession turned me on, I had to draw the line somewhere.

This time, it was better than to let her have her way with me. Our rendezvous would have to continue somewhere else.

"I won't talk to you right here, Essence. Legend can come out any minute and then our secret will be out."

"Rain, I love you. I was good enough to be your wife at one time and I hated you for what you did to me, but now I love what I've become. Nevertheless, I feel you should make me your Queen."

I took a deep breath and pushed her up against the tree firmly. "I'm not feeling any of your shenanigans. You're taking this too far."

She whispered in my ear, "I'm your secret."

We stared one another down and the rage in my eyes told her I would fight her if I had to. We would fight 'til death.

Suddenly, Legend came outside. He sensed trouble and shot me a confused look. There was no way I could hide Essence any longer.

"What's going on out here?"

Essence said, "Hello, Legend. It's good to see you again. I was just—"

"She was just leaving."

She smiled widely as if to say she wasn't going anywhere. Legend was paying close attention to the way I had her pinned against the tree. I had a grip so tight that my nails were digging into her skin.

I ordered, "Essence, take your ass home."

"Oh, now you want me to go home. Is it because Legend is standing here? The other night you were deep inside of me."

I tightened up my grip on her arms and she laughed loudly.

"Tell me she's joking," Legend said.

"I wish she were joking, but she's telling the truth, but that has nothing to do with her stalking me. She even stalks me in my dreams. She can manipulate dreams. That's something she's perfected."

Legend frowned a bit and replied, "I know... The reason why is she's trespassed into mine as well."

Essence continued her laughter. "Did you enjoy me in your dreams, Legend?"

I stared her down. What was she trying to do? Was she trying to play my own brother against me?

"I don't disrespect you the way you are disrespecting me, Essence. Stay out of my family's way. You hear me?"

"Or what? You might as well kill me now, Rain; this is only the beginning."

This had been coming to a head and it was time to pop it. It had been red and aggravated long enough.

"Now isn't the time to talk about this," Legend replied. "Our parents are on their way. You need to get rid of her right now."

"Hey, Legend, tell Rain the truth. He needs to hear the truth, finally."

"Shut your mouth," Legend replied calmly.

"Who was the vampire that I slept with? Hmmm?"

I let go of Essence's arms and turned my attention to Legend. This was splendid news. "Is she suggesting what I think she's suggesting?"

The look on Legend's face told it all. He'd slept with my wife and broken our bond. He'd betrayed me. That's when I did the unexpected. I punched him in the face as hard as I could. We were fighting, wrestling all over the grass.

Essence saw my parents pulling up with Azura, so she fled the scene. Azura screamed for us to stop. Father tried to jump in the middle.

Father hollered over us, "Chill! Rain!"

"Legend slept with Essence and you want me to chill? How could my own brother betray me this way?"

"Calm down."

"You knew about this?"

Confusion set in as I stared at their faces. They knew. My head started spinning. My own family was aware this whole time. I didn't have any facts, but I was left to assume that Legend had seduced Essence when she was vulnerable.

"There's no need to get upset, Rain. We did what we had to do for the family," Father asserted.

"If my brother wouldn't have made himself available to my wife, she wouldn't have broken our bond!"

Legend said, "It was only going to be a matter of time, brother. She's in love with me, too."

I started walking away. I didn't have anything to say to any of them.

Azura was on my heels. "Rain, please don't be mad at me. What Legend did was necessary. Essence was taking control over you in a way that we've never seen before. You would've never stepped into your rightful duties."

"You were in on it, too?"

"Yes, but…I love you, brother. We all love you. We were trying to protect you."

"If that's what you call love, then I don't want it. Essence was going to be the only woman I was going to love forever. You wonder why Essence has crossed over to the dark side. It's because of the betrayal."

"That's not true."

"Azura… Essence was my wife."

"It was always your wife this, and your wife that! Rain, it's over. We will get over this. Can you forgive us?" she asked with tears in her eyes.

"Not right now."

She turned slightly away from me so I couldn't see her tears. "I hope you don't stay away too long."

A light bulb went off in my head. Did they plant Olivia in my life as well? "And this thing about Olivia… It was set up from the beginning, but she's also a piece in your little game of chess, right?"

"Yes."

I cocked my head to the side trying to figure her out. It was easy for my family to control everyone, especially me.

"Does Onyx know about this, too?"

"Yes."

"I can't believe you all would deceive me… I need some time away. I don't want anyone coming to look for me. Stay away from me."

She didn't respond. For the first time ever, Azura didn't have a smart comeback for me.

I ran as fast as I could; at the speed of light.

It was hard for me to look at Olivia when I made it home. I could tell that she had heard about what had happened. I was sure my mother had called her. While I paced the living room, she watched me nervously.

"Your mother wanted me to ask you if you were okay."

"Oh, is that so? Just like she asked you to come back from New Orleans to make me fall back in love with you?"

"She wanted me to be here for you to keep your mind off Essence, but it didn't work." Her face turned very serious; her blue eyes seemed cold all of a sudden. "I know you're a man. Many women have loved you throughout the centuries. I also realize how hard it is for you to be who you are, but I believe you fell for me honestly. I could've left you and you wouldn't have known where I was, but I'm not cruel. I really do love you."

In the back of my mind, there was still that provocative question. "Did you only want to be with me because of the Divination?"

She thought about it. "I already was in love with you before I knew about the Divination."

"Did you use any of your powers to force this?" I raised my eyebrow.

She shook her head, looking hurt. "No."

"I just discovered that my own brother broke my bond with my wife, my parents coaxed him to do so, and you are guilty by asso-ciation."

"Your family has always been overly protective. You can't blame them. Rain, you are destined for greatness. Ulysses will walk in your footsteps. Together, you will take over Pigalle Palace and put things the way they should be. You can't be mad at Legend for protecting that."

"Legend had no right. They don't know what would've happened if he didn't corrupt Essence. He ruined her. I didn't create that beast on my own."

"I wish you could look at it from their standpoint."

"What do you want from me, Olivia?"

"Have I ever asked you for anything other than love?"

"No."

"I stayed. Even after I found out you were still sleeping with her."

She came to me and placed her hands on my face. "I truly am in love with you. Our spirits are connected and I want to be your Queen."

"I believe you, but you have to understand something. I can't love you the way you want me to love you right now and honestly, I don't think you have what it takes to be the Queen. You let my Mother manipulate you. She will only manipulate you some more once you're in power."

"I understand. I don't blame you for thinking this way. I will be gone before dawn. If you want me, you'll come for me."

She pulled away from me to pack her clothes. I stared out of the window. Drops of rain trickled from the dark clouds. A storm was brewing.

CHAPTER 35

ONYX

"Lovebirds," Azura said as she entered our home with Mother, Father, and Legend.

Soleil and I were in the middle of sharing an intimate moment of kissing.

"You two are so cute," Mother stated.

We parted and I asked, "Where's Rain?"

"Onyx, Rain knows about Legend and Essence," Azura replied.

"And how did he find out?" I questioned.

"He and Essence have been seeing one another and this evening, she followed him to Legend's place. During a confrontation, she decided to tell Rain while Legend was standing there."

I took a deep breath and rubbed the lines that were forming above my brows.

"I thought Rain knew already," Soleil said.

"If Rain had known, he wouldn't have been calm about it," I replied.

"Oh."

"Soleil, you look so good," Mother complimented to change the subject. "Where's my grandson?"

"He's sleeping in his room. I can take you to see him."

"Is that a diamond ring I see?" Mother asked, lifting Soleil's finger.

"Yes, Onyx proposed."

"That is gorgeous, Onyx," Mother cooed.

"You have good taste," Azura added.

"Thank you."

"I want to see the baby, too," Azura said, following Mother and Soleil to the nursery.

"Did you try to explain to Rain why you seduced Essence?" I asked.

Legend cleared his throat, rubbing the back of his neck. "I couldn't get a word out. He attacked me."

Father said, "We're going to let Rain have some time to him. Thankfully, we have Olivia there keeping an eye on him."

"How much longer do you think he's going to allow her to be there with him? Especially if he feels ambushed by the family. He's not going to trust Olivia," I pointed out.

"True," Father said. "We'll have to wait and see."

"What are we going to do if Rain decides he wants nothing to do with us?"

"We're family. He has no choice," Father answered.

"When is he going to be crowned?"

"Next week sometime."

"I'm sure the Préfet can't wait to have him take the throne."

"You do realize that once Rain is King, he can make any decision he wants," Legend said. "He can decide to never allow any of us into the castle."

"Rain wouldn't do that," Father replied.

"We don't know what Rain will do," I said.

"How are you feeling, Legend?" Father asked.

He answered, "I'm okay. Look, I'm not proud of sleeping with Essence, but from here on out, she can no longer come between us."

"You haven't been still sleeping with her, have you?" Father questioned with suspicion.

"No, but she's been in my dreams. Rain says that she manipulates dreams. Let's say, I've let her have her way in my dreams..."

"If Essence can manipulate a dream, then the more power she gets, the more she will be able to do in dreams," Father said. "I believe Rain has learned a good lesson today. He has to get her out of his system and the first step would be to keep her out of his dreams. The same goes for you, Legend. She can do some damage if the two of you let her."

"So, I must've given her more power by allowing the fantasy to play out in my dream?" Legend quizzed.

"Without a doubt. Her plan is to destroy this family, starting with you and Rain."

CHAPTER 36

LEGEND

I checked my voicemail as soon as I got home from Onyx's place. The family meeting was long because we really had to come together on our next plan of action. We didn't want Rain to start pulling away from us. We were going to have to let him cool down. I loved my brother with all my heart. I didn't want to hurt him the way he was hurting. I was hoping to hear his voice on the recording, but he hadn't called.

Essence's voice came through the box before I could settle in, and the sound of her stopped me dead in my tracks. "Legend, this is Essence. I want to know if we can meet up and talk as soon as possible..."

Why did she want to talk?

I called her back without hesitation to see what she was possibly thinking with what she'd done earlier that day.

She picked up after a few rings. "Legend..."

"Essence."

"Do you think you can swing by my place to talk?"

"We only have a few hours before dawn. I don't want to risk it. Can we talk over the phone?" I asked, checking my watch again as if I hadn't already looked at the time.

"No. I need to see your handsome face."

"Can you meet me here, then?"

"I'm on my way."

She hung up. I didn't trust her to meet her at her place. What if it was a setup or ambush? Essence was going to have to behave in my home.

I tapped my fingers against the side of my jeans and put my dreads in a ponytail. All the while, I couldn't help but feel as if I were making a mistake by allowing her to come by. I stared at my front door with my mind reeling. I popped my knuckles, took a deep breath, and rubbed my face before I straightened up. She knocked on the door.

I opened the door after a few seconds.

Her sweet fragrance greeted me. She had her hair in big curls, her face was natural without any makeup, and she had on a white tank top without a bra. I could clearly see her hard nipples. Her short shorts accentuated her wide hips as she turned to enter the room. Her legs were oiled and silky-looking.

Poison.

I kept my composure and took my eyes off her luscious-looking body.

"Thank you for allowing me to see you." Her voice was like music to my ears.

From the first time I lay with her, I understood why Rain was so crazy about her. Something magnetic drew me in.

"So what's up?" I asked.

"Let's sit. So, we can make ourselves comfortable."

We sat on a cream-colored loveseat and I made sure I sat on my side without touching her. I could tell by the color of her eyes that she had something up her sleeve.

"So what's up?" I repeated, keeping a stern face.

"I have something very important to tell you."

"You came to tell me that you are done stalking my brother and that you won't be entering our dreams anymore."

"I can assure you that I won't enter your dreams, but I will never stop stalking Rain," she replied with a sly grin.

As soon as she said his name, I felt my temperature rise. I didn't want her trying to come between us any more than she already had. "What do you want with Rain?"

She handed me a piece of a golden medallion of some sort attached to a thin necklace.

"What's this?" I asked puzzled.

"This is what he gave me when he turned me."

I shifted in my spot. "What is it?"

"That's what I want to know. He hasn't told me. He said to keep it in a safe spot. It's something your birth mother gave to him at a young age. Rain has the other half."

I went in my memory to think about the necklace Rain wore. From what I could make out from my memory, it was very similar to the piece she was holding.

"He's been wearing that necklace around his neck for as long as I can remember. It has sentimental value because he almost lost his mind when he thought he lost it once. We all figured it's a piece of jewelry that he treasures. Why would he give this to you?"

"I'm not sure, but I think it's a key of some sort when the pieces are put together."

"That's a very odd-shaped key. Why do you think it's a key?"

"An educated guess."

"That's not enough for me."

"Look, I called you tonight because I thought you would know something about it. Rain is hiding something very important and I want to know what it is. Don't you?"

I stared at her with a deep frown, causing my brow to wrinkle. Desperation was on her face. "You want me to help you?"

"Yes…"

"This doesn't make any sense. Why would Rain trust you over any of us?"

"Maybe it's because he knew you all would betray him and his judgment. He chose me for a reason. Before he met me, he knew that I was right for him. Rain has more power and insight than he lets us in on. I'm sure he knows exactly what's going to happen before it happens. He's a Daywalker and because we don't know any, we really aren't aware of what kind of powers he has. Your birth mother passed on something to him that he has kept with him for centuries. He took his time to search high and low for a suitable wife. You must not tell your parents about this. This is something I want you and me to work on, together."

"My parents have to know. If they think I'm betraying them in any way, I will be disowned. As the oldest son, I have to remain loyal to my family."

"Does it bother you that Rain is the youngest son with these powers? Do you ever get jealous?"

"Of course I get envious, but it is what it is. I respect the Divination."

"You respect it so much that you were willing to sleep with his wife to go against him?"

I felt my anger rise. She was pushing all the wrong buttons. I stood up on my feet and yelled, "I think it's time for you to leave."

"Why are you getting so upset, Legend?" Her voice was calm as she eased her hands around me to sit me back down next to her. "You must gain your brother's trust. You must find out what he's been hiding. As the oldest brother, your right is to be aware. Why did your mother never pass this on to you? You were the first-born son. She didn't know about the Divination, did she?"

"She was murdered before the Divination was revealed."

"Do you see my point? He was chosen as a favorite from the day he was born. Why is that? Your mother was a human. She had no powers, right?"

I stared at her with skepticism, but my mind was racing. Refusing to fall for a trap she was trying to set, I replied, "Well, I can't help you 'cause I have no memory of anything that happened before I became a vampire. None of us do."

"Rain does."

My insides were starting to boil. Rain never let on that he had any memories. He rarely talked to us about much, and now it seemed as if Essence knew more than the rest of us. That didn't sit too well with me.

"You should leave, now."

"But, don't you want to know what this is and what it unlocks?"

I was very curious, but I was still confused. "If it is a key, why do you want to know? How will this benefit you?"

"I'm not sure whom it can benefit, but Rain does. Rain said to keep it in a safe place and I have a feeling that it unlocks something in that palace."

I took a deep breath. I didn't want to be a sucker for her, but for some reason, I had the weakest spot for her.

"I'll try my best to find out what I can." I was waiting for her to say thank you, but the thought hadn't crossed her mind. "Has he asked for it back?"

"No. That's the strangest thing. He hasn't mentioned a word about it. It's almost as if he knows I'm coming back to him."

"Maybe he forgot that he gave it to you."

She shook her head, crossed her legs, and bounced the right one over the left.

"I doubt that," she replied.

"Are you going to stop fighting your feelings and go back to him?"

"I love Rain. No one will ever make me stop loving him."

I shook my head at her and folded my arms across my chest. "I can't believe you would feel that way, even after we've been together. If there's any way to make me jealous, that's one of them."

"Is that because you want me?"

"You're crazy... or maybe I'm going crazy."

She laughed at me. "I know the truth, Legend. I've been in your dreams, remember? I didn't have to trespass, as you so called it. You called me in, didn't you?" She scooted closer to me.

"I did, but..."

"Legend, you can't stop thinking about me. That's what bothers you the most, isn't it?"

I dropped my head, feeling lightheaded, confused, dazed, and stuck. She was trying to get into my head. She had already gotten into dreams and made it feel so real. The cruel game she was trying to play was actually working, probably better than she planned. I chewed on the inside of my jaw, thinking, looking at Essence, and wondering if all of this were a bad dream.

"You don't cheat on people you love, and you for damned sure don't sleep with their brother."

She rubbed my arm and then placed a soft kiss there. "I'm sorry if I couldn't resist your strong arms, your smile, and your dreads. What woman can resist you, Legend?"

Though I knew she was stroking my ego, I allowed it. "When I came to you that night, you were so afraid and so lost. You didn't understand why Rain did what he did to make you belong to him. I took full advantage, but you opened up for me, willingly."

Without hesitating, she replied, "I needed you. From the moment I laid my eyes on the both of you, I fantasized about having both of you at the same time."

I let out a good laugh. That was funny. It wasn't like Rain and I hadn't shared women in one bed before, but the thought of his beloved wife sharing a bed with his brother at the same time was ridiculous.

"Essence, you're so beautiful and you know that."

She grinned sexily. "You came to me, Legend, and now, we are both guilty for the sins that we've committed."

"Why did you have to tell him? It could've stayed our secret."

"You threw me off. Seeing you...him...standing there. The look of surprise on your faces... The whole thing threw me off."

"Here I am, hanging on to your every word. How do I know this all isn't a setup? How do I know you're telling the truth about the medallion that you think is a strange key?"

"Why haven't you ever paid attention to the necklace that's around his neck?"

"I haven't. Once I find out more about this *key*, then what?"

"Find out more and then we will go from there."

I wished she hadn't come by. It was only to talk about Rain. I was hoping I could get inside of her again. The feeling she gave me when I came was a feeling I had never experienced, but it was time to let her go.

"Is there anything else you want to talk about?" I asked.

She sat in my lap. Her passion penetrated through me as she stared into my eyes. She kissed me easily and I didn't protest as both of her hands took hold of my dreads.

"Take me tonight."

The temptation was there, but I refrained and stood my ground. "If you truly love my brother like you say you do, and you truly want to be his Queen, then you need to stop this madness. There's still good inside of you, Essence. I see it. Go to Rain and you make it right with him."

Tears came to her eyes. I continued, "Marry him. When you are Queen, he will reveal what that key unlocks. That will be the only way to find out."

Easing off of me, she smiled as if she were proud of me, as if I had passed some test she had given. Her tears escaped her and cascaded down her cheeks.

"That's very noble of you, Legend. Your love for your brother is deep. You only came to me because that's what your parents wanted you to do. You make things right with your brother, too."

"I will. Be good to him. Be good to yourself."

After placing one last kiss on my lips, in a flash, she was gone.

CHAPTER 37

ESSENCE

It wasn't hard to find Rain. He was sitting in his home, waiting for me. It was amazing how he could sense when I was coming. That's how I knew our bond was deeper than we both wanted it to be. I wasn't going to fight my feelings any longer. I was madly in love with Rain. I didn't want to harm him and I didn't want to see anyone cause any harm to him. Even if he would've never been crowned King, my feelings would've still been the same.

I fought against him because I was afraid of what I was becoming. I was afraid of my power. I had to get out in the world and experience everything I could about being a vampire. The good, the bad, and the ugly. To be honest, I didn't enjoy hunting down innocent people and ripping them to shreds. Their blood gave me a rush, but I wanted to have more control over my ill thoughts.

Being with Rain was my destiny.

He didn't acknowledge my presence in the room as he stared out of the window. I wasn't sure how to start the conversation, but looking at him, I could tell that he was a changed man. He was more confident, more handsome, and had the demeanor of a king.

"Sleeping with Legend was a mistake," I said. "I'm sorry for hurting you. I'm here to beg for your forgiveness, Your Highness."

He remained silent.

I floated over to him and fell to my knees before him. Placing my head in his lap, I cried. I cried real tears. What I felt inside was something I had been fighting far too long. I discovered that I could control the dark side and I wasn't going to live without Rain again.

After a few moments of my tears soaking up his lap, his hands touched my head.

I looked up at him. "Rain, I want to fix us. I want to be with you."

"Why?"

"Because I love you."

"I know you love me, but can I trust you?"

"You can trust me."

"What about your brood?"

"I let them go a while ago. They no longer follow me."

"Good." His caress was gentle as he continued to stroke my hair. "You have to promise me that you'll put your complete trust in me. You must not work against me."

"I'll be by your side through everything for an eternity."

I was being sincere and honest. The hatred I held, I let go. I put the key out of my mind as well. Once he put the puzzle together himself, he would be able to tell me what the key unlocked. Since he couldn't trust his family, I was all he had.

"What's going to happen to the family?"

"I made a decision that I feel is best. From now on, everyone will have to do what I say. Only I know what's best for Pigalle Palace. They have to learn the hard way that no one stands between us."

"I hope your mother and father will finally accept things."

"Don't worry your pretty little head about them. I'll deal with them. My job is to protect you. No one will bring harm to you."

"Does this mean that we're getting back together?"

Rain stared at me hard and he read my thoughts in a flash. He smiled once he could see that I was telling him the truth. Both of his hands cupped my face. When his lips met mine, his kiss gave me the answer.

CHAPTER 38

RAIN

Essence and I were crowned the day after our wedding. My family attended and nothing seemed to make me happier. Château de Chambord was now reclaimed as our royal house and all was calm in the streets of Montmartre.

On our very first night as King and Queen, Essence and I spent the night alone.

"Let's go for a midnight swim," she suggested.

"We can do whatever you want."

After she changed into her bathing suit, she noticed I was still in my clothes.

"Aren't you going to swim with me?"

"I don't really like the water, but I'll watch you."

She giggled and took my hand in hers while we walked down the corridor. Once to the pool, she jumped into the water. I watched her poolside. Essence looked soft and angelic, much like when I first laid eyes on her. She was finally all mine. She was my Queen.

When she was done swimming, we sat there, basking underneath the moonlight. Her hair was wet and hanging past her shoulders. Little droplets of water sparkled before dripping off the ends of her hair. Her amber eyes sparkled as brightly as the droplets of water.

Her nipples were hard and poked out against her wet bathing suit. I could barely see the darker color of them beneath the white material, but I had memorized the way they looked. I looked back up at her face and that's when I realized that she was gazing at me the same way.

Not a word was spoken as we leaned toward one another.

We stared into each other's eyes before allowing our lips to touch. It was a soft kiss—a kiss of love, not one of sexual need.

We were finally together.

I brought my hands down her sides, feeling her figure as I kissed her chin. She threw her head back, allowing me to kiss her neck. I licked the water droplets from her skin, tasting the sweetness of the water and the slight saltiness of her skin.

I was aware of the bats flitting about overhead and the splashing water fountain before us. Essence moaned and I began untying her bathing suit. She reached up and gently pulled my head between her exposed breasts. Feeling her hands on the sides of my face, her touch was so sensual. It was a touch of love. Her fingers slowly made their way to the back of my head as I moved my mouth to her right nipple.

Once again, I heard her moan, barely audible over the gurgling waterfall as I grasped her nipple between my lips. I felt the hardness of it against my lips as I slowly slid my mouth around it.

I don't even remember her hands leaving my head, but the next thing I knew, I felt her lifting my shirt and I leaned back so she could pull it off over my head. She threw her shoulders back allowing me to remove her bathing suit completely. I looked down and saw how her breasts stood out. They suddenly became hard from the slight breeze of the night's air.

I licked the water from them and tasted her skin again.

She put her hand against my forehead to stop me. She wanted me to look at her. She wanted me to remember how she looked at that moment. The first night she was legally my wife. Therefore, I did just that before I kissed the ends of her fingers.

Focusing on her nudity, I stared at her exposed bellybutton, and then back at her breasts. I saw how her collarbone glistened in the wet sheen the spray of water had left. Then, I looked at her neck, her chin, and full lips. I looked into her eyes once more and knew I was right. It was what she wanted.

She could see that my dick was hard and ready to fuck her until she couldn't take any more, but we were going to make love that night. We were going to explore each other and make love right there, poolside with the waterfall in front of us.

She pulled my swim shorts down while staring at me with pure love and acceptance in her eyes. Once I removed my shorts, I climbed over her. She sucked my tongue when I slid it between her lips. She lifted her chin when I nibbled on it. She arched her back as I kissed first one, then the other nipple.

I licked my way down her body and bellybutton. I sucked at her skin just above her mound. I kissed her knees, licked her ankles, and kissed the ends of her toes. When I looked up at her, she slowly spread her legs, exposing her most secret parts to me.

I was going to taste her, savor her womanly nectar, her essence.

She moaned louder as I dragged my tongue along her inner lips. She gasped and pushed her pelvis into me as I penetrated her deepest parts with my tongue. She moaned even louder when I gently blew on her clit. I covered her sweetness with my warm mouth, and when I pushed my tongue against her clit, she couldn't help but orgasm. I left her with no other choice.

Again, we found ourselves staring into each other's eyes. It was easy to see what she wanted. She wanted to feel me inside of her, but first, she wanted to touch me. I will never forget the soft touch of her wet hand over my manhood. She felt it. She gently squeezed it along its length. She pulled me forward and gently placed a kiss on the end of it. I had to fight to keep from coming as I watched her open her mouth. I watched as inch after inch sunk into her soft mouth. For a few moments, she pleasured me. When she was done, it was time for us to join as one person.

We both knew it.

I looked down the length of her nudity. She was beautiful, much more than words could describe. I slowly moved myself up and down her clit. I loved the way it felt and the way she closed her eyes, I could tell that she did, too.

I was entranced by her.

She was still.

I was still.

We listened to our quickened breaths as I made love to her nice and slow. We felt the moon, shining down on us, and we both were aware this was a moment that could never be repeated the same way. This was a unique moment in both of our lives.

Then, savoring the moment, each time I went inside of her, she drew a sharp gasp. Inch after inch slid into her until I was at the very bottom of her sex. It was as much as she could take. Our union was complete. We were now one again. I continued moving in and out until her gasps became moans.

We shared an orgasm.

When she opened her eyes, she looked at me, and whispered, "I love you, King Rain."

They were the first words that had passed between us since we lay underneath the moon.

"Queen Essence, you possess a beauty that is worth pursuing, a beauty worth fighting for, and a beauty that is core to which you have revealed to me. Your beauty can be felt and it affects me. I made the right decision."

Her hand carefully traced the gold half-medallion that hung around my neck.

"I still have the other half," she said.

"Good."

"What is it?"

I stared at her carefully. "My mother told me it's a special key. The two pieces, together, unlock something here in this castle. I don't know where to look. She said it only works with two people, one male and one female. She specifically told me to give one to a woman whom I would spend eternity with and when the day comes, together, we will unlock something."

She frowned and replied, "If your mother was human, how did she get this? Does anyone know about this?"

"No one knows, but me. My mother was human, yes, but she was born to King Allemand and Queen Christione."

She gasped, "So, you were destined to be the heir anyway."

"Technically, Legend would've been the next heir, but the curse rearranged things."

"And your mother was human?"

"Yes."

"Born to vampire parents?"

"Yes," I replied.

"How can a human child be born to vampires?"

"It was a birth defect. They hid her from the Préfet and sent her to New Orleans where she grew up with a human family that King Allemand trusted. When she met my father, he was a vampire. Because she knew all about her parents being vampires, she was instantly attracted. She stayed in her human form and gave birth to the three of us. Once word got out about her half-blooded children, they murdered her and my father. She already knew her destiny because she had powers. Though she was human, she had supernatural powers and could cast powerful spells. Her father, King Allemand, gave this medallion to her and he told her to pass it on to her youngest son… He was the one that wrote the Divination."

"Does anyone else know that you are King Allemand's grand-children?"

"Mother and Father know, but my siblings do not."

"All this time, Rain, you've known that you're a direct descendant of King Allemand?"

"Yes. That's why the Divination was written. Allemand knew he and his wife would be killed. He knew his daughter would be killed. He had to leave something behind so the government could make sure that only his heir would rule Pigalle Palace once again. Their bodies lay in a hidden tomb, somewhere in this palace."

"Your mother's body, too?"

"Yes."

"Do you plan on telling Legend, Onyx, or Azura?"

"I will tell them when the time is right. There is so much more I can say; only I'm uncertain. While I'm here, I'm going to find out everything there is to know. I want you to lay back and enjoy tonight. There's no need for you to worry about these matters."

"I'm ready to go inside. Will you be joining me?"

"Yes, my love."

ABOUT THE AUTHOR

Born and raised in Sacramento, California, Niyah Moore was touched at an early age of nine with the precious gem of prose. Under the subtle pushing and guidance of a literary mentor, Niyah decided to pursue a career in writing professionally.

Her works include novels, *Major Jazz, Guilty Pleasures, Bittersweet Exes, Pigalle Palace,* Tell Yo Bitch series, Suckcess series, Nobody's Side Piece series, and *Beneath the Bayou.* She is included in several anthologies such as *Zane's Busy Bodies: Chocolate Flava 4,* Anna J's *Lies Told in the Bedroom, Heat of the Night,* and *Mocha Chocolate: Taste a Piece of Ecstasy.* She is also an Honoree of the 2013 Exceptional Women of Color Award of Northern California. Niyah is a mother of two, who loves sharing her love for words with the world.

She currently resides in Sacramento, California with her fiancé and two children.